For E and D

Hope you enjoy it!

All the best!

Gary

ONE

What compelled me you ask? Why, in the solitude between these four walls, do I sit in guilt stricken grief, ravaged by my own internal demons?

The answer is simple. Necessity!

I could tell you that I had recently undergone a massive psychological trauma, my wife and kids had left me. I lost my job, I was forced to sell my home and live in the squalor of 'bedsit' accommodation.

I could say that I had dabbled in drugs, and, over the years of abuse I had spiralled into an oblivion of paranoia and self disbelief. Or even that I was suffering from a mental illness, that didn't manifest itself until my later years, and I hadn't taken my medication.

If I did tell you these things, I'd be lying. I'm not married and never have been. I don't have any kids, at least not ones I'm aware of, and the closest I've come to drugs is half a drag on a friend's spliff. Even that half of a drag made me cough and splutter like an idiot, and made me decide never to try again.

No, the reasons and the why fore's aren't a complex structure of emotional and social influences, as I expect some expert paid a fortune to think about these things will assume. I wasn't suffering stress, and my childhood had absolutely nothing to do with it.

Knowing the answer to your question however, isn't quite as simple as it first seems. Agreed, its not thoroughbred conundrum, but there is a story that comes with that simple word. If you've got the time I'll tell you all about it.

I always think the best place to start is the beginning, so that is where I'll begin.

TWO

In the dying embers of the summer of 1975, my bald, naked, wrinkled and crying self was born into the world. I've been told that the summer was hot, and my pregnant mother had had quite an ordeal carrying me. A couple of weeks premature my early few months were a constant headache for my loving parents.

I wouldn't eat, barely slept and would cry without showing any sign of relenting. At times I'm sure my parents wondered exactly what they had done, having this life changing creature. This must have been especially so in the early hours, with work pending and my crying keeping the household awake.

The good news is that things got better.

Home was a three bed semi on a quiet little estate just outside the city of Wolverhampton. As a matter of fact, of all the places I've lived in my life, and there's been a few, that three bed semi will always be home.

My father worked hard for a living, seven days a week he toiled in a steel mill, totally and utterly devoted to the family, his hard work kept the roof over our heads and food on the table. I will always appreciate everything he did for me.

As a baby, and in fact during my entire childhood, I wanted for nothing. We weren't rich and perhaps I didn't have the latest toys or the latest fashion clothes. Even though, wearing a padded body warmer, riding a brand new BMX would have been nice. Still, really I wanted for nothing, I was satisfied, content even happy with my lot.

As the years passed the family grew into a very close bunch of people, we loved each other dearly. Mom and dad were the perfect couple. I never once heard them argue, there were never doors slammed in anger, raised voices and certainly no swearing. Dad wasn't a drinker or a smoker, and neither was mom, there were no vices, and you could say that it was the perfect family life.

As you can see, things are going swimmingly, my childhood, up to school age was perfect, I couldn't have asked for anything more, and I wouldn't change it for the world.

I'm not going to bore you into turning to the last page to find out what happens, by giving every single piece of trivial information about me growing up. I expect you want to hear the good stuff, what's happened to get me where I am now. I'll give a simple, terrifying, and completely terrible word that explains my next few years.

School.

The best years of your life. Well, mine was barely eventful. I was a good student, worked hard, knuckled down and at the end of it all managed to get mediocre grades. I was the typical average student, never really excelled but by no means any kind of failure either.

I wouldn't say I was bullied; OK, I wasn't Mr Popular but there were quite a few kids a lot worse off than me. Being a bit of a short arse and weighing in at barely ten stone I wasn't the sporty type either. Stripping down to a pair of shorts in the middle of winter never rated high in my 'lets do things fun' list.

On the subject of height and weight, I never really grew much after school. I spurted to five feet eleven then stopped, and despite eating anything in sight, I never put any weight on either. As you can see, I'm still the same today.

I know what's coming next, seeing as I'm not a man mountain, how did I manage to do the things I did?

Well I'll let you on in a little secret. If you put your mind to it, anyone can do anything, and a lot of the time people just aren't expecting to die that day.

They always think there's another day, and they'll always get home later that day. Well frankly, that's just not true.

THREE

I couldn't tell you exactly when it was, what month, day or even year, and it's not like it's something I'd lusted for over a period of time. It was just a fact of happen chance and something inside that clicked.

I can honestly say, hand on heart, it was, every single time premeditated.

The first is always the best, maybe it wasn't at the peak of my prowess but it's the one I'll always remember; The one that rolls over in my mind, the face that haunts me, the harbinger of my guilt.

I think it's the price of modern society, fast paced, everyone wants immediate service and nothing can wait. I was the victim of the service industry. I sat, everyday beneath the luminescent glow of the office lights. My computer, which incidentally required more attention to keep working than anything else in the office, gave me the information.

I'd spent, nay wasted, an entire week of my life learning how the computer system worked; I was its slave, nothing came from me, I was the voice of the computer. The call centre in which I worked was the 'beating heart' of a major life assurance agency based in Telford. I was lucky, in the fact that I didn't have to work shifts, some poor souls had to man a 24 hour hotline.

Why is it that no-one can wait until morning to ask their questions? Why do we need to have someone employed around the clock, in case someone 'needs' the information at half past two in the morning.

Anyway, I digress.

The day was pretty much the same as many others I'd had. At twenty six, I was in a dead end, I had just been speaking to an obnoxious caller who disagreed with the computer. As the go between for the two I had it in the ear from both sides. The computer was relentless in its decision, and the caller could not accept it, I was using the time to think to myself, whilst offering agreeing and disagreeing grunts at the appropriate moments.

One of the only benefits of the job was Jane. Jane sat next to me and also fielded calls from obnoxious callers. Jane was getting married but every now and then I'd catch a glimpse of her leg as she moved and her skirt opened at the split.

I'll make one thing clear, I'm no pervert and through this story you'll hear no evidence of rape or anything similar, so if you think that's ever been part of what I do, and feel disappointed that I'm not, I'll save you the pain of reading the rest of these pages. However, I am male, and twenty six, and yes, that is blood running through my veins.

Jane was petite and blonde and although not stunning, she was attractive, and if she wasn't getting married I would have asked her out at some point. Well I like to think I would, I'd probably just be happy with the odd glimpse of leg now and then though knowing me. I'm not going to kill Jane if that's what you're thinking, I actually really like her, I wouldn't want to kill her.

Jane had just inadvertently shown me a glimpse of leg, she had nice legs. Being petite she had a slim frame and I imagine had naturally shapely legs. It was around this time I got to thinking, I'd read a lot of murder stories about the ways and means. I'd read a couple of Agatha Christies Hercule Poirot the master murder detective, let's face it, those little grey cells always got the man.

Murder, how easy would it be to murder someone? Personally I didn't think I had the balls, not just because I'm afraid of blood or anything like that, but because generally I have such a regard for life, and respect for other people. My dad taught me that.

I'll let you in on a little trade secret, black tape. Black insulation tape, can work wonders, black gaffa tape can be useful too, all in all black tape is a good friend.

So what was the big deal? "Yes sir" I said to at least the third Mr Obnoxious. "I completely agree, however looking at the final surrender value you will have a far greater return going full term." The computer told me the information.

"I'm not a trained financial advisor sir, I can only work with the information I'm provided with." The computer gave me all the information, and as I've already said, the computer's decision was final.
I mean how hard is it to kill someone and get away with it? Are all murderers caught?

It was here talking to at least the third Mr Obnoxious that the first premeditation began. I use premeditation in this sense in the loosest of terms. At this stage I had very little premeditation, but it was there, eating away at me ever so slightly.

I had the plan in my mind from an early time, in fact there were a couple of times that I had considered doing it, then bottled out at the last moment. I'd taken the time to do all the preplanning but when the moment arose I'd simply pulled out. It was here, at this point that I doubted whether I really had the balls to do anything like this, oh how wrong I was.

I'll go back to the black tape, whether it's a strange co-incidence or the fickle finger of fate, but the width of black insulation tape is almost exactly the same width of letters that make up a car registration plate. So much so, that my car registration is quite easily adapted to something that by no means resembles its true identification. Three small tears of insulation tape is all that is needed.

I'd driven around a couple of times with my precariously altered number plate, when I stood back it was quite convincing, at least I knew the speed cameras would never catch me. Like I said, there were a couple of times the thought had flashed into my mind at the right time, but I'd bottled out.

You might be quite surprised about what I'm about to say, and you may think, what a load of shit. Something like that would never happen, but believe me, in a crisis people are like rabbits, they freeze as if caught in headlights and can barely remember anything about what has happened before their eyes, especially when it grates against everything society has taught them about behaviour.

So its five thirty pm, and I 'm driving home, I'm not talking about the three bed semi home, this is my two bed starter. Thin walls, so thin that I can hear my neighbour sneeze, and flush his toilet at some ungodly hour while I'm trying to get some sleep.

This is the first place I can call mine, ok the carpet doesn't match the paint on the walls and 'The House Doctor' would admit the place into 'house hospital' straight away, but its mine. A place for me to come and reflect, and drink beer, the only thing that keeps me sane.

Five thirty, should it be that things happen on the hour or every half hour afterwards, I don't know, but it was five thirty that it all began.

FOUR

So I clock off out of work at five pm. The office works a flexi-time system, so as long as I'm in early enough the rest of the week, come Friday I can do best part half a day.

Its Wednesday though, and five pm. I push my personal card into the clocking system and it beeps me out of the office, oh what joy that beep means. I take a wander down the steps and into the foyer. The car park is only a five minute walk away, and luck being a lady tonight Jane has finished at the same time, I walk with her to the car park.

I talked to her about the day and ask her why she thinks people who call into us think we're some kind of Nazi dictator wanting to take their money, when really we are just people doing a job. Five minutes passes quickly, and soon Jane is in her car heading towards her fiancé.

I look at my car, both the front and rear number plates have been altered using black insulation tape. It's amazing, an F is so easily turned to an E, an L is so easily turned to an E, or a P so easily turned to an R. I wonder what Hercule's little grey cells think of that.

I get in the car and start the engine, the power of the 1.6 litre Ford Mondeo springs into life. It's amazing what a weapon a car can be in the right hands. Despite planning what I wanted to do, I never really thought I was going to carry it through. The moment of change was like something inside that clicked, and I had decided I was passed the point of no return and had to continue.

I didn't really see her until about five seconds before I made the decision. The West Midlands Travel bus had pulled over at the side of the road and she was walking past the bus trying to get to the other side of the road. I had plenty of time to see her, and to be honest the braking distance was well inside the 'Highway Code' margins. Still, something inside me clicked, and I set in motion a sequence of events that I couldn't stop.

I only marginally slowed, enough that when my bonnet hit her just above the knee, it pushed her forward carrying her legs away from her. I saw as her head hit the bonnet.

Her arms and legs seemed entirely individual from each other, one arm was thrown behind her, with the other looking as though it was protecting her face, and her legs looked as if she was about to do the splits.

She landed on the tarmac with a thud, my screeching tyres bought the car to a stop exactly as I thought it would. There was a stagnant harmful smell of burning rubber, a smell not associated with heavy breaking but a smell associated with wheel spinning, like a teenager from traffic lights.

I was shaking and if someone had of spoken to me I would have stammered every word. I walked to the front of the car and looked at her. She must have been only seventeen, she had long dark hair, and could quite easily have passed a course in modelling.

Although now she would need extensive dental and surgical help.

At this point my mind was clear, despite everyone else looking on with their mouths open and hands to their faces, I walked straight up to her and picked her up, put her over my shoulder, like a fireman would carry an injured person down a ladder. I opened the boot to the Mondeo and slammed her inside, she started to stir so I hit her against the head with my Krooklock, blood started to flow from the unconscious head. I got back into my car and drove away, straight onto the M54.

Its strange, but I read from the newspaper the next day, the third person point of view. It was a dark car, the registration plate came back to a milk float - entirely a coincidence. The man was in his twenties, average height, average build, dark hair wearing dark clothing. From over twenty witnesses, that was the best

13

they had to work with. That description could be one of thousands of people in Wolverhampton alone.

Lets face it, I had never been arrested. My details were not in any ongoing investigation, hell I didn't even have any points on my driving licence. Whatever evidence they found could not directly be linked to me. The only thing was her.

I pulled over in a side road and opened the boot. She lay there, terrified in the boot of the car. No-one was around so I punched her hard into the face, with as much force as I could muster. My god, the pain was terrible, I thought my hand was going to explode. Stalone didn't feel this much pain surely.

I don't know whether she realised that she would be dead within the next 25 minutes, but she certainly knew that this wasn't meant to be happening to her. I didn't really want to mess around too much, there was a big part of me that thought I was going to get caught, and the fear made me finish her life quickly.

I'm not really a big fan of gore, and I honestly hated this part of the job, but unfortunately it had to be done. As time goes on you'll see how I change this, because not only am I not keen on the gore, but its messy, and blood is incredibly hard to wash out.

Anyway, this was the first one and all of my premeditation wasn't complete. I had managed to use two electrical ties to bind her two hands at the wrist, and her feet at the ankles. I had used black gaffa tape across her mouth, this didn't really have the effect I expected, she was still quite loud, its just I couldn't quite make out the words.

I looked down at her blood smeared face, she had definitely been pretty, she had a well defined face, high bone structure on her cheeks. She had a pleasant face to look at, well it *was* a pleasant face. The one I was looking at was somewhat blood stained, but as I said, I will never forget that face.
She was out of the boot of the car and was kneeling on the ground. I imagine she was begging, judging by the drones of her mumbles and stifled crying. Either way, I couldn't stop now.

The claw hammer slammed into the side of her skull with an ear wrenching crack. It was the kind of sound that sets you're teeth on edge, like fingernails down a blackboard. I winced at what I had just done to this girl's head, but I knew it was a matter of necessity. Probably the worst blow was when the claw part of the hammer got stuck in her cheek bone, when she rocked as I swung at her face. I had to hold her forehead to get it out.

That face was now horrid, I've never seen so much blood before, it seemed to keep flowing and flowing. The hammer was drenched and I was splattered by it. I could see though, that the eyes were turning bleak and life was slowly escaping her. I didn't want to cause any more damage, but I knew I should deliver one last blow to make things quick for her.

The last blow caught her directly on top of her head, the hammer caused a nasty dent in the skull, and now I could see that her eyes were staring blankly out at her surroundings, nothing was going on inside.

My first murder was complete.

FIVE

There were a couple of things about that first one I hadn't accounted for, obviously due to inexperience.

Firstly was the blood. By the time I'd driven away from that side road, I'd left her in a massive pool of blood. Not only was the pool incredible, but I was covered in it too. My hands and my clothes were drenched, it took me ages to get the blood off the steering wheel following the drive home.

Secondly was the damage what I consider to be a flimsy body makes to the steel of a car. There was a nasty dent on the bonnet where her head had collided with it, a dent at the front where I had impacted on her knee, and the bumper was scratched quite badly.

A couple of days later though and £250.00 down the drain at the local garage and the car looked as good as new. This murder game was expensive, and if I was going to continue I needed a better job, or a long time from one to the next. I opened a savings account at my bank later that week.

I can't explain exactly what I felt during that first one. It's like describing a taste, you can't do it without relating it to another taste. Anyway, like I said earlier, there was a certain amount of horror. Also a dreamy disbelief that what was happening wasn't real, I almost felt I was a stranger looking out of my own eyes.

The intense feeling of the adrenaline was almost in stark contrast to the dream like feeling. The colours were sharper and I could hear and smell things I probably wouldn't have normally.

You may or you may not know this, but blood smells. I don't mean if you cut your finger there's a certain smell, but I'll tell you, when there's enough of it, out in the open, you can smell it. Almost as if the smell becomes a taste, there's a smell/taste of the iron, and a musty type smell that I can't explain. The adrenaline increased the senses, but it still felt like a dream.

Then there was the overwhelming feeling of power, power of life and death. I suppose, looking back at things as I am now, there really wasn't any power. I mean, there was no way I could have let her live without facing a long spell in jail. Irony.

I still felt it at the time though.

On the first night afterwards, I had no chance of sleeping. I sat downstairs with the television on, staring blankly at it.

I asked myself all sorts of questions. Had I really done it, when were the police going to knock the door, and that face. That once beautiful face, destroyed. All the life, smiles and personality behind it lost into the ether forever. All her dreams, all her past. Memories, times on holiday with her parents, her first kiss, the first time she had sex, what she wanted to be after college or university, even what song she was going to sing at the karaoke at the pub Friday night. All these things were now lost forever more, and no-one, no matter what was done or said could ever bring any of those things back.

I suppose my guilt started then. I'm not a terrible man, and I still believe I'm not. I know, my actions at some points in my life say otherwise, but deep down I am kind and gentle. There may be a few times during these pages you will seriously doubt that, and I will certainly understand. In fact I imagine you already doubt it. Before you hang me without trial though, there's a whole lot more I need to tell you about me and the things I do.

So what are you thinking? Sickened? Do you feel sorry for her or for me? As you know, this isn't the last time something like this happens, and no, I don't get caught right now, let me tell you about what happens next.

SIX

There was a media frenzy to start with about her. It didn't take long for police to figure out that the girl knocked down in Telford, and whose body had been taken away by the driver of the car that hit her, was the same girl found in a quiet side road in Essington, just outside Wolverhampton.

I remember a police officer making a statement on the news. He must have been important, his cap was braided and there were crowns and pips on his shoulders. He spoke with a very posh accent, an accent that truly fitted him being a high ranking officer in Staffordshire Constabulary.

"..this is an horrific attack on an innocent young woman. We are currently following up enquiries and would welcome any information from witnesses to either incident. There are a couple of people we wish to speak to in order to eliminate them from our enquiries. We make an appeal for the driver of the vehicle to come forward." There was no way I was going to do that. The news presenter went on to ask a couple of questions and then gave a 'hotline' number for any witnesses.

Let's face it though, news moves on fast, people want to hear of death and destruction daily. The same old stuff gets boring after a couple of days. The majority of time though, all the death and destruction is only a gimmick to keep 'the great unwashed' out of the things that really matter. Interest rises, how much they are paying for a litre of petrol, that a politician has been involved in fraud, even that their rights are being taken away by a new European law that no-one has a say on, death and destruction keeps all these things off the front page.

The next day I was in two minds about what to do. I thought, if I went into work people might find it suspicious, especially as I still had all the dents in the bodywork of my car, and I looked as though I hadn't slept all night. Which obviously I hadn't. I called in sick, proclaiming a terrible and paralysing bout of the tummy bug, and that I was barely able to get off the toilet.

Incidentally, I was having a bit of a problem in that area, I can only put it down to the stress of the day before.

I used the day and arranged to have my car fixed. I was a little bit worried that the garage may catch onto the damage and put two and two together. "Dow wurrie abart it." he said in a thick Dudley accent, and I knew I was safe.

I know that the guilt was still there but I was able to put it to the back of my mind for the time being, there were things I needed to do, just to make sure the police didn't come knocking.

It was about three or five days later that the media made reference to her, it was probably the first time I took a real note of her name, age and life. The regional news began with the story, and I've got to be honest, I cried about her.

"Emma Jackson, an 18 year old University student of music and drama, was the victim of a horrific attack on Wednesday. Her killer, initially knocked her down as she got off a bus heading towards a charity entertainment show at a university campus in Telford. It appears the driver of the car kidnapped the injured Emma, drove her 15 miles along the M54, where he got off the motorway, pulled over in a side road and brutally murdered her with a hammer."

A lump was in my throat already, now came the punch. Her teary eyed, sobbing and begging family appealed for anyone to come forward with any kind of information. They were desperate. They had lost a loving daughter, who had aspirations of being singer or actress and was a popular and honest student. They said she would be sadly lost by the entire family and everyone who knew her.

I had taken her away from all of those people.

One of the amazing things about being human is the ability of self preservation. I knew that to even mention anything about either the road accident or the hammer attack, would leave me open to enquiry. So really it was quite easy to stay quiet about everything. It was important to me to realise that if they police had any real leads, they would have followed them up by now. I had expected them to be at my door before now, and looking at what evidence they had, the prospect of them knocking my door was not going to happen any time soon.

I want to be clear about myself. I'm not an idiot. I'm actually an intelligent and articulate man. It might be an idea to go back to another part of that 'growing up' I skipped over earlier.

After achieving, what I consider to be shit 'A' Level results I went on to university in Wolverhampton. Whether this is coincidence or not I studied Applied Biology, which involved a great deal of human anatomy, genetics, and biochemistry.

So, now having watched CSI on television, and knowing what I do about DNA and the body in all its beauty, I know that my DNA was all over Emma corpse, when it was recovered by the Scene Of Crime Officer. I mean I'd struck her head seven times in total with the hammer. I'd tied the electrical ties and placed the gaffa tape across her mouth. My DNA was everywhere. The only problem was, that without my profile already on record, any confirmation of what DNA had been found was useless. The DNA profile that they received at the office came back with the same answer - 'No Trace'.

I'll tell you something else about criminals as well. According to 'experts' Offences such as murder and rape are very rarely committed by people with no criminal past. They say that these offences are usually committed as a progression from things such as serious assault (Murder) and a variety of sexual offences such as indecent assault or exposure (Rape).

Someone like me very rarely comes along. I say this because someone like me is a complete headache for whatever police force I happen to be in at the time, the last thing the police ever expect to deal with on their territory is a serial killer without any identifiable motive.

I've always found that things come to me quite naturally, I've never really had try hard at anything. I imagine I could have excelled in almost anything - except maybe art (which I am terrible at). So through school and university, I muddled my way through doing the bare minimum. I will say this though, when I hear things they stick.

Things have always been the same. I'm not really shy, but I never really put myself forward for anything. This has a strange kind of effect on people around me, because I don't put myself forward people assume I've got nothing to say. This is fine by me because that generally means that people underestimate me, so I'm safe in the knowledge that I'm generally one of the more intelligent people in the room, while everyone else is underestimating me. This becomes a lot more useful as time goes on.

Being at university gave me a thirst for knowledge, and I could often be found in the library looking up subjects that interested me. Not really to improve my grades, because I've never been obsessed with what grades I've got, but for my own personal satisfaction. This quest for knowledge meant I was quickly very good at researching a particular subject. I found I could glean information from a variety of sources and put it all together to make much more sense. My ability to dissect information also becomes very useful as times goes on.

The good thing about being a Biology student is that you have to undertake practical sessions, these vary from dissections to a laborious sessions trying to get a particular colour in a test tube through filtration. I remember I turned up to my first ever practical session a little worse for wear through beer. I hadn't bought any of my books with me, or my lab coat, the doctor leading the session asked me if I actually belonged in the class. First impressions last.

University life was fantastic. Due to my quietness I was never very popular at school. I came out of my shell a little at University - Not all the way, just partly. It did open my world to women and beer though, both of which play a massive part in my life. Like I said though, I'm no pervert, I just find myself completely engrossed by women, and have not always treated the ones I've known with utmost respect. There's an easy explanation for that though - I'm a man.

I'll tell you a bit more about the women of my life a little later, if there's time and you want to hear about it - you may not. For now though I just want to push forward and move on in my life, and how I recover killing Emma Jackson.

SEVEN

The two days I had off work sent me onto the weekend, so at least I had a couple more days off before having to go back to Telford.

I picked my car up early Saturday morning, and it really was a very good job, there was no sign of an accident at all. The mechanic had made some small talk with me while I was paying and he was writing a receipt. He talked about the killing of that poor girl, and I'll tell you, my heart was in my mouth. If he'd have eyed me suspiciously I would have bolted out of the garage right there and then.

How inconspicuous that would have been.

Luckily the guy was just making small talk, and he quickly moved on to talking about Wolverhampton Wanderers.

Despite the Ford Mondeo being one of the most popular models of car in Britain, I felt somewhat exposed driving around in it. I mean, this was the car that was my major weapon in killing Emma, and I'm driving it around like there is nothing wrong.

I know it sounds a little paranoid, thinking that my car, of all the cars out there that could have matched the one described, would be picked out. It is something that ate at the back of my mind though. I took a detour on the way home and went to speak to the bank.

Isn't modern day society amazing, people actually pull you're hand off to give you money, my bank were grateful that I was borrowing money off them, and within the hour I'd arranged a loan, with the clear intent of buying a new car.

I bought a copy of both the Autotrader and Exchange and Mart, and routed through them both for a new car. It wasn't as easy as I first thought. I discovered that I had a few things that were a 'necessity' in my new car. For example I didn't want to waste valuable time and energy having to wind my windows down, no, I wanted electric windows; and a sunroof. Fog lights would be nice, and it should look pretty good too. I didn't want it to be too old, but didn't want to spend the entire amount of the loan either.

I needed a new suit.

As you can start to see already, things quickly turn into a hierarchy of necessity. The next most important thing overrides the one before, and luckily for me, this leads to those things that bother you most being pushed aside.

I can't speak for everyone when I say this, but I found that the death of Emma, although obviously never leaving me, was pushed to one side, then eventually right to the back, while I made decisions, that basically kept the police from my door, and made me feel better about myself. I don't know if this is an ability that everyone has, the ability to cope with severe anxiety and pressure by putting it to one side and concentrating on something else, but it definitely worked for me. I suppose I never would have found this out having not done what I had, so rightly, not many people will know if they can do it or not, if you're interested, and want to find out for yourself whether you can do this kind of thing or not, take a word from the wise.

Ignorance is bliss.

So I was ready to start looking for a new car, and the following Saturday after Emma's death I was at a car lot looking for my next car. I'd seen a few things in the Autotrader, but when I'd given them a call, they had already been sold. So I decided to do a tour of the local garages and see if there was anything there that took my fancy.

There's one thing you get used to when buying a new car, and that's the patter of the salesman. They always do their very best to get you the best possible deal they can manage. They say that if the boss new exactly what they were offering they doubted they'd let them offer it to you.

What a load of bullshit.

After making at least a thousand pounds on the car you are using in part exchange, the salesman then makes another thousand pounds on the price of the car you are buying, because lets face it, its not often you come across a car of its year with such low mileage in such good condition. It really makes me laugh that they can say these things to your face and keep theirs straight. I can draw a slight comparison here to them and me, I can keep the truth from others, and my face will never waver.

That Saturday was completely frustrating, I'd been to at least seven different garages and not found anything similar to what I was after. I was tired and my feet had started to ache. I am always the same when it comes to looking for something. I get it into my head about what I'm after, and if I don't find it, it annoys me and I get frustrated. I feel I've got all this money burning a hole in my pocket and I'm desperate to spend it, but can't.

I decided that I needed to treat myself to a night out with my friends. I'm not really a party animal, but when I go out I make sure I have a good time. Before the night had begun I had no idea exactly how good the night would be.

EIGHT

I had a close circle of friends, and despite starting to get older none of us had settled down. We started the night as usual in the Crown and Cushion Pub, it was usually a quiet place, which meant we could have a sit down and chat, before the drunkenness set in too deeply.

Before long however we found ourselves, as usual, at The Civic in Wolverhampton, flinging ourselves around in a semi-dance to a whole host of now ancient music, long out of fashion. There were seven of us out that night, a good mixture of boys and girls, which made sure that those of us (myself included) still single, had enough attention from the opposite sex.

I've never really had any problems attracting women. I'm by no means a stunner, and no-one has ever swooned over me, but I still manage to get my fair share of attention.

Just like Emma, I will always remember the first time I saw Melissa. Me and my mates were dancing in a group, almost excluding outsiders. I look up and saw a girl looking over at our group. She had long blonde hair, just past her shoulders, and a face I could look at for eternity.

She caught me looking at her and our eyes met for a moment, before I looked away, I waited a couple of seconds and took another look, we were looking at each other and our eyes met again. I gave a slight smile that she returned. I continued dancing with my mates.

I left it a couple of minutes and looked over to where she'd been dancing, to my slight disappointment she was gone. I thought about it for a moment, and whether I should have gone over to her, but was soon handed another can of Red Stripe lager by Chris, my closest of all friends.

I had known Chris from the first year of secondary school, and we'd been friends for the best part of 15 years. He was the one guy I knew I could depend on, and tell almost anything to. Emma, was the only thing, so far, that I had truly kept to myself.

Myself and Chris were very similar in character, but he was a lot taller than me, but just as slim, it gave his height an appearance of more than it was, simply he looked slightly narrow and awkward. He had never murdered anyone though, at least not to my knowledge.

Anyway, I'm sure I'll spend enough time talking about Chris later, tonight is about me and Melissa.

As you have no doubt guessed, as I call her by her name, and have already said that tonight was a good night, that I see this girl again, and that her name is Melissa, at this time, on this night though I don't yet know this.

The can of Red Stripe that Chris had handed me, had only lasted me 20 minutes, and I was then motioning to Chris, by tilting my cupped hand to my mouth backwards and forwards, asking him if he was ready for another drink. Chris gave me a nod, and I went off to the bar.

There was a throng of people trying to get their hands on more alcohol, and I was at the back. It took me a while to manoeuvre myself into a position to be able to place an order. I was stood, with my elbows on the bar, awaiting my turn. I looked to my left and there she was, standing right next to me. She must have felt me gaze, because she looked straight at me.

I can't remember exactly what I said to her, but it made her laugh, I noticed then that she had a lovely mouth and smile, she reminded me of someone off television, but I couldn't quite place who. It was my turn, and I ordered a couple of cans of Budweiser, completely different to what me and Chris had been drinking all night, but I was confused and at a brain loss in her presence.

It was only a minute or so, but we were talking to each other no stop, I paid for the two cans of beer without even noticing. If the bar maid had forgotten to give me my change I wouldn't have noticed. To be honest, I don't think she did.

So I am standing at the bar, with two cans of Budweiser, talking to Melissa, but I don't even know her name yet. The conversation was mainly drowned out by the music, but we still managed to seem to get on, and our conversation was peppered with bouts of giggling from both of us.

I walked with her back to the dance floor, and by the time I reached my group of friends, I quickly handed Chris his can of beer. He looked at it and frowned at me, a glimpse of stark realisation soon hit his expression when he saw Melissa by my side. He held the can up almost above his head in what appeared to be a salute, and I turned back to Melissa and gave her a smile.

At the bar, the music seemed to drown out almost everything about our conversation, right now though, I could barely hear the music. It was me and Melissa, dancing together. I could hear every word she said, it was right at this point that I heard a word that had a meaning like no other word I knew. It was a word which would come to describe things that here and now, standing in a crowded club, I could never imagine. It was a word, that would come to define a whole plethora of emotion for me, it would describe the high points of my life, my comfort, my life, my love, my home, the word was simple.

Melissa.

Her name resounded in my head, I didn't want to forget it or release it. We continued to dance together, and the time seemed to fly by and before long, the last song of the night was on. A slow one "For all the lovers out there". I danced close to Melissa, and half way through the song we began to kiss. In a blink of an eye the lights were on and we were alone on the dance floor, still kissing and members of the club security staff had to separate us and shepherd us out of the club, me and Melissa were happy to be led out, holding hands.

We stood outside the club for a while and kissed again,

Melissa's friends soon turned up though and dragged her away to get a taxi, we exchanged telephone numbers before they did though, and I walked around the corner to find Chris waiting for me, with a greasy burger in his hand. Everyone else had gone home, but Chris had waited, so that I didn't have to get a taxi home on my own.

I talked to Chris for a while, who wanted to know the ins and outs of the night for me, but he soon changed subject and we headed towards the casino, to finish the night with a spot of roulette, black jack, and a cheap taxi home.

During the taxi ride home to my house, where Chris would crash on the sofa, I fell asleep, only to be woken up by Chris at my front door, fumbling for change for the taxi and for the keys to get me inside.

The next minute or so felt like a marathon, as my drunken self attempted to get the key into the lock. It seemed that every time I moved the key up, the lock moved down. I closed one eye, in order to aim the key better, but still managed to miss the lock. In the end, I held the key against the door and moved it up and down, left and right, until the key met the lock and slid inside. I turned the key and opened the door to my house.

I can't remember going to bed, or talking to Chris, or even making the cup of tea we both had. The next thing I really remember is the early morning Sunday headache, and squinting at the light coming through my bedroom windows.

That Sunday was pretty much like any other day after the night before, except that I arranged to meet Melissa again later in the week, and had to try and find a replacement for my 'suspect' car.

It was probably mid-afternoon by the time Chris and I were ready to go out and about looking for a new car, as far as Chris was concerned, I was just unhappy and bored with the 'family car' Mondeo and wanted something newer and more sporty.

Now I had been to a few garages yesterday and hadn't been able to find anything, but one thing that Chris and I share is a tendency to enjoy looking at and for cars. Luckily as it would be Chris knew of a couple of garages that I had missed out and we decided to go and have a look for a replacement for the Mondeo. As we headed out I wasn't entirely sure I should be driving, and hoped I wouldn't be stopped by the police, that is the last possible thing I could want.

The first garage that we tried was a complete dive, the best car on the lot was worth £1000.00 and it was a rusty knacker. After arriving Chris looked at me and we laughed to each other at the ridiculous cars on offer. I was starting to worry that my money was going to be whittled away on beer if I wasn't careful.

Ten minutes drive towards Wolverhampton though, on the outskirts of Wednesfield I came across a garage that I had forgotten had existed. I pulled up outside and we got out to have a look around. There were a few decent cars, and there were even a couple out of my price range, and I liked the look of both. I have an expensive taste that my budget doesn't match.

In the second line of cars though sat my new car.

I'd looked at the two cars that I couldn't afford, just for the sake of it, and there was only one other car that I fancied on the lot, it was a mark one Toyota MR2, it was getting on a bit, but the bodywork was good and it hadn't got too many miles on the clock.

As we were looking around it, Chris gave me an approving glance and I went and picked up the keys from the portacabin office. Back at the car I opened up, sat inside and started the engine. It started nicely and sounded great. It was strange having the engine sat behind me, it gave the car an entirely different feel to anything else that I'd been in.

After another half of an hour and a fair amount of car juggling on behalf of the garage owner Chris and I were driving around Wednesfield in a white two seater sports car and we were loving it. As you can well imagine, it didn't take me long to fall in love with the car and there was no option about whether I was going to be having it or not, especially when it was well within my budget.

Upon our return to the garage and the welcomed delight on the garage owner's face at having the car returned in one piece, we got out and discussed terms. Trading my Mondeo in and coming to a mutual agreement on price, which ended up being £250.00 less than the price on the windscreen, and the deal was done. A handshake sealed it.

Despite only having a 1600cc engine, the MR2 was surprisingly quick, to this day it was probably one of the most fun cars that I've ever owned. So I've gone from one of the most inconspicuous family cars, a dull green Ford Mondeo, to a 'look at me' white two seater sports car, talk about a complete change for the opposite.

In many ways, Chris helps me through my life, and is involved indirectly in a few of my murders, I'm going to go into more detail about all that later, I think its about time though that you start to hear about murder number two.

NINE

Before I go any further I need you to understand that although the next murder had a motive in mind, and it was Melissa, it's not necessarily what you think. By the time I commit my next murder you should know that everything between me and Melissa is going great when it takes place.

Another key point in murder, www.com, oh yes, the internet is a massive resource where people are taken at their face value, and money talks. Anything can be bought and sold, and almost anything is for sale, at the right price.

My motive for this murder was one born out of frustration, like I said, don't get me wrong, everything between me and Melissa was going fantastic, but every now and then, or more often, Emma would creep into my thoughts.

The answer was simple I naively thought, I needed to replace Emma with someone else. I needed not to have to see her in my mind, instead I decided the best thing to do, would be to kill someone else, but not be as involved as I was with Emma. I wouldn't want to know the name, age or any personal details. I'd try and remove myself from the death completely.

My thoughts turned to murder, and soon I was thinking about it during every moment of my spare time, when I wasn't faking being happy at work, or loving being with my friends, family or Melissa I was thinking about what to do, whether it was while driving to work, sitting on the toilet, or more often lying in bed awake waiting for sleep to come.

There were two main objectives to my thinking.

Firstly I wanted to be free and able to live my life as usual afterwards, without being confined to any prison, let's face it, that would be the first objective of any of my murders. Secondly was to keep myself free of the media surrounding my next murder, to relieve myself of Emma. This would be harder to achieve than the first objective incidentally.

Again, whether it is co-incidence, fate, destiny or something else, I don't know, but while I was hard at work thinking about how it could be done, the eventual final plan came to me with very little time to spare. The ideal time was almost upon me, and all I needed to do was finalise the exact place and wait for the moment.

The internet, a buyers market that becomes more and more useful as time goes on. I'm not usually in during the day at home, so anything I have delivered from the net I send to my parents home, and yes, its still exactly the same house I grew up in. After a few flicks with the mouse, and a Paypal payment direct from my account for $49.00, the order had been placed for a key piece of my murder. OK it wasn't quite legal, but that was the beauty of the net, if needs be I could claim ignorance, but that really wasn't necessary.

Merely a week after the order from the USA, the package arrived, I picked the package up from my mom on a Tuesday afternoon and took it back to my house for closer inspection and to familiarise myself with its operation.

I couldn't have asked for anything better, it was the perfect size. I strutted around my living room and kitchen wearing my jacket having it concealed in the right hand pocket, it fitted into the pocket well and felt just the right weight and size in the palm of my right hand.

Holding it my hand gave me a sense of security and power.

Just outside the town of Willenhall at a place locals call New Invention and near to my family home is an area of woodland, the name escapes me right now, if you were to ask my brother he'd tell you the name straight away, but right now I can't think of the name.

Anyway, it was here I decided it was going to take place, the plan was set in motion. All I required was the right time, this took patience. Waiting is not my best quality, but one which I become accustomed to.

It was mid February and we were experiencing a worse than average winter, which was much to my liking. We had had a heavy falling of snow overnight. I looked out of the window after getting out of bed and saw the snow, my heart was in my mouth.

I called into work and left a message onto the answer machine that I wouldn't be in today, apparently even the switchboard and reception hadn't been able to make it in today.

I dressed appropriately and headed out in my car, it was slow going as there were not many people around, even so it only took ten minutes to get to the woodland car park. As I pulled into the car park I saw a red Vauxhall Astra estate parked in the car park already. Fresh tyre tracks spouted from the back wheels of the car, as it had obviously recent pulled into the car park.

I parked near to the car and headed into the woodland. Judging by the footprints in the snow, added with the fact that the Astra had a metal gate above the rear seats separating them from the boot meant that at least one dog was being walked.

I looked at the prints and if there was only one dog it was excited.

I checked the object in my right hand pocket, its weight and feel in my palm gave me the confidence and reassurance that I needed. I locked the car and headed off into the woodland. The snow crunched beneath my booted feet as I followed the excited dog(s) and owner prints into the woodland. I walked for a few minutes and decided to stop and take account of my surroundings.

Things always seem to happen fortuitously, as I was standing taking in my baring I heard the familiar noise of an excited dog. I waited for a while as it became close and closer, the whimpering and stifled bark alerting me to the oncoming victim.

I want to say a quick word here. Panic. This single word comes into play a whole lot.

It was only a couple of minutes before a long haired Collie dog came bounding around the corner of the trees to where I was standing. The dog halted in its progress and took in my smell. It was a little nervous to start with, but with a little encouragement and a few strokes with my left hand later, it was quite happy with me. As I was stroking the dog, which incidentally looked a lot like Lassie, the owner turned the corner of the trees. I took a moment to measure up my victim.

The dog instantly bounded away from me and to its owner, greeting him with a leap placing its front paws on the owner's belly. He was about forty five to fifty years old, he had greying hair that had once been a vivid black, he was about 6'2" tall with a stocky build. I was surprised to see that he wasn't as well wrapped up as I was, granted he had a waterproof jacket, but it wasn't a padded insuled thing like I was wearing. He was obviously used to being in cold weather.

I noticed that no other dogs appeared as he got closer.

As he approached the dog came back over to me and I gave it a stroke, my mouth was dry and I was running through my mind about what I was going to do and say when he got to me.

As I stood and spoke to the man I was shaking, I suppose he could've put this down to the cold, but it was my nerves, he was taller and stockier than me, and if this didn't work I was in for a proper brawl with this guy (which I didn't fancy myself coming out on top of!)

I started talking about the dog and the weather, and if anyone else was out today. I agreed that only the stupid like us two would be out on a day like today. Now comes a moment that I mentioned earlier, just as when I had driven into Emma and onlookers had gawped at us with open mouths and hands on their faces. Panic.

I pulled the object from my pocket and held it so that he could see it. "Do you know what this is?" I asked as his gaze was fixated upon it. I pushed the button and it crackled into life, a brief moment of realisation flashed across his face, then I jabbed the object into his ribs, just below his left armpit.

The stun gun delivered a whopping 500,000 volts into him.
Judging by the instruction pamphlet I was to hold the device on
the subject for a maximum of 5 seconds, anything over a second
would knock him over.

Five seconds is an eternity when you're engaged in doing
something like this to someone.

Now just like with Emma a couple of things happened that I
wasn't expecting, lets face it, it wasn't like I could've tested this
out beforehand. Firstly the guy became suddenly rigid for a
moment and gave out a high pitched yelp, this didn't last very
long though, I held the stun gun against him as he started to
topple. I found that by the time he had fell into the snow I was
still holding the gun against his ribcage and I was half straddling
him. Secondly by the time I realised I was done with the stun
gun I noticed he was lying in a patch of yellow snow, he had
pissed himself. Yuk!

I looked down for a moment and he was shuddering in a
spasmodic dance in the snow, completely unable to take control
of his muscles. The dog was going crazy around me, it was
jumping around, barking and snarling. I discharged the gun into
it too. There was a brief smell of burning fur before it dropped
into the snow, I didn't know if it was dead or not.

I got to work straight away, I grappled with this thrashing guy as
I packed his mouth and throat with snow. This wasn't as easy as
I thought, luckily he was in no mood to bite me, but it was
taking all my strength, concentration and effort to get the snow
into his mouth. Even a barely conscious body doesn't want to
suffocate to death.

Getting the snow into his mouth was only the beginning, I got
my glove caught on his teeth a couple of times, it was the
thrashing and struggling that I found hard to cope with. As the
life ebbed away from him, as he was unable to breath or clear his

throat, the body became extremely violent. It took all my strength to keep his arms and legs pinned. I was aware that I was sweating, despite being surrounded by snow.

As the struggles subsided, I stood up and again took in my surroundings. I realised that I could have had an entire audience of people watching me and I wouldn't have noticed, I was so engrossed in what I was doing to this guy. I was out of breath and the sweat was pouring down my back. A strange sensation when you're surrounded by ice and snow. The dog wasn't far away, but I decided to leave it where it was. I dragged the body beneath a crop of trees and loosely covered it with snow.

Somehow in all the action I had managed to remember to put the stun gun back in my right pocket before I'd started struggling, I don't remember the actual moment I did it though. I looked around, steadied myself and headed back towards my car.

By the time I reached the car park I had regained my composure and my breathing was under control. I noticed that mine and his were still the only two cars in the car park. My tracks and those of my victim and his dog were the only ones leading away from the car park too, as luck would have it we had spent our time together completely alone. Hopefully, by the time his body was discovered all that would remain would be the footprints, tyre tracks and the body, that's if it was discovered before the melt. If not, there'd be nothing but the body.

I got into my car and gingerly drove it away, I was a lot more careful on the return journey, I wanted to make sure that there were no accidents, I wanted there to be no record of me being anywhere near here.
It took me an extra five minutes to get home, there was a slight flurry of snow during the journey, but nothing serious, I was soon back in the parking bay outside my house safe and sound.

I went inside and made a cup of tea.

ELEVEN

Rough Wood, that's the place, I knew it would come to me eventually, my brother would have told you the name much before now, but better late than never.

After an initial bout of arguing with him as kids, my brother and I enjoy a fabulous and close relationship, not in a taboo brotherly love way, but we are as close as the best friends of anyone you could name, and then some.

These places I can remember due to the massive impact they have on me, sometimes though it's a matter of hitting the right synapses. As you will come to see, as I progress and in order to avoid a lot of suspicion, I take breaks into a major city which will all become clear in the fullness of time, you can then take into account the full extent of what I have done.

As I look back on my life, with the things that I've done to other people and what I've left for those that survive; as I'm here, waiting, it makes me think about the prospect of what will become of me after my own death.

I have to admit I'm not much a believer in life after death, even so, when the time comes, I'm going to have those last rites and repent all the same, I'm not that proud and want to edge my bets! I just hope that I'll have time to get it all off my chest and fit all the Hail Mary's in before my time is done.

Personally I think that heaven and hell exists here on Earth, lets face it though, if there is an after life, I'm off to the latter. I think that I have experienced my heaven, the time with my family and friends, being on a roller coaster with Melissa, watching the sun go down on the ocean from Crete with Melissa at my side. Playing games as a kid with my brother, going on holiday to Paignton with my family as a child. Moments of elation and joy, shared with people who love me. Heaven.

You find me now in my own personal hell, haunted by faces, the knowledge of my crimes and the fear of what may be following my own death, there's quite a story left though yet to get to where I am now.

If I quickly go back to what I've just done, and the fortuitous circumstances that I found my victim I'm bought to think about fate, destiny and coincidence. If it hadn't have been for Emma, things never would've been how they are today. Let's face it, have you ever slammed a hammer into someone's skull so hard that their eye socket cracks, and the eye bulges beneath the skin?

I often think about the co-incidences that took place for me to kill Emma. If she had been late getting up for instance, or even if she had sat near to the rear of the bus which would have meant she'd have got off seconds later, I would have missed her. Everything came together at the perfect time, which makes me wonder whether I really had to decide what to do, if there really was a choice, or if destiny plays more a part of our lives than we care to think about.

All this talk of destiny, coincidence and the afterlife is again sidetracking me from the things I need to tell you about, how I'm almost caught, the next things that I do, and how I get to do them, my life is a tangled web and we're only scratching the surface. I know, two people are dead already, but we're nowhere near the end, not even half way.

TWELVE

I sat at home with that cup of tea staring at the television for hours. The tea was cold before I put the cup to my lips and I couldn't tell you what programme was being shown because I wasn't taking anything in, it was time for my mind to repair the damage I had just done to it.

Things like this usually happen when you sleep, your mind takes account of the day, puts things in perspective and keeps you sane, exceptionally I had to do this before sleep, the amount of irrational behaviour I had to explain to myself required extra work than a nights sleep. Again though I managed to put what I had done to one side after a few hours, and before long it was at the back of my mind.

There were still the odd glimpses of Emma though.

I saw Melissa later the same day as she travelled to mine, despite my best concerns and advice over the danger the trip involved especially in the snow.

We spent the rest of the day in front of the fire watching a DVD, cuddling on the sofa, I can't remember what the film was and to be honest, it doesn't really matter. The snow and coldness was trapped outside and we were warm and snug together. Like I said, its times like this that are my favourite, nowhere to go, nothing we have to do, simply enjoying each other's company.

You might ask yourself how I manage to do this, and looking back I can see what your saying, but I have to say, at the time I was able to rationalise things, I wanted these times with Melissa, and I wanted to enjoy them without interruption.

Neither Emma nor the guy I'd just killed was anywhere near my thoughts.

I couldn't have asked to be with anyone better than Melissa, she was considerate, honest, loyal and the most beautiful woman in the world in my eyes. No matter what other regrets I have, I feel truly honoured to have spent so much of my life with her.

She would be wonderfully insightful, sometimes if I was going to be home late, I'd pull into the private parking bays outside my house to find her car already parked there. Despite working all day herself, she would come to mine and make us something to eat for when I got back. Heaven. In my own way, for no reason in particular, I'd turn up to her house carrying a bouquet of flowers. No matter how long we'd been together these private gestures of love never ceased from either of us. I can see that was one of the things that kept us together and things so great between us.

I have always thought that a key part of a happy relationship is to do favours for each other, rather than expect or demand something. That and to try and keep the people you have killed out of your head.

Despite what I said about the guy I killed, the very next day I half expected to catch a glimpse of something in the news about a local body, but nothing at all. I don't regularly buy a newspaper, so I wouldn't know whether anything had been in there. I carried on regardless.

In fact, it was three days before something was mentioned on the news, and it wasn't that a body had been found, as the snow hadn't melted yet, but rather that a local man was missing. Nothing further, for an entire day, before it was all over the local news.

I didn't really recognise the story at first, as it wasn't what I'd expected. Like I've said, when it came to details, I always tried to make a cup of tea or go to the toilet, anything that didn't give me a name.

What seemed to be enthralling to the media, more than anything was the dog. Apparently, a man who had been walking his dog had suffered a heart attack in the woodlands, his dog had stayed by his side, and it was obvious that it had made attempts to waken its owner due to how the dog and the man had been found.

This didn't make sense to me at first, I'd left the dog quite a way from the man, why would anyone think that it had been trying to wake its dead master?

There wasn't a photograph, however it was described that the dog had been found nuzzling the man's head. Clearly I hadn't killed it with the stun gun. The dog had made all attempts to wake its owner before the cold became too much for the dog, despite hunger, the dog had made no attempt to feed off its dead owner, preferring instead to die next to him.

Why were all these people surrounded by such sad stories?

So, it was a heart attack responsible for the death? At least no-one would be looking for the murderer this time. That was the one thing I had in my favour. I thought.

Things aren't always as they seem, as you'll see time and time again, and have no doubt seen already, but for the time being, I'm going to leave that vague sentence as that, I'll come back to it later.

It was quite easy to carry on to be fair, I knew I was safe, I had cleared the most of Emma from my head, and the guy who replaced her I knew nothing about and was distant from.

I had achieved exactly what I'd been hoping for, I was free, and more than that, no-one was looking for me. I knew nothing about him and was able to put all of my thoughts and desires into Melissa. Ok, there was the odd moment, I'd wake up in the middle of the night and find myself thinking of either Emma or him, but that wasn't very often. Much more preferable to the way I had been with just Emma under my belt.

It was at this point that I felt truly at home with Melissa, I decided to treat us to a night and meal out such was my buoyant mood. I didn't really have much money, but I had a savings account, and $49.00 wasn't as much of an expense as I was expecting, so I had a bit left over to treat Mel.

We booked a table at our favourite Italian restaurant; I wasn't bothered about drinking and drove us there on the evening, we'd got ourselves dressed up, we liked to put extra effort for each other for something special and out of the ordinary. I wore a nice shirt and trousers and Mel was draw dropping in a black dress that came down to just above her knee. Looking at her made my mouth water more than the smell of the minestrone soup I'd later eat.

THIRTEEN

Remember what I said about things aren't always as they seem, well I'm going to come back to that in just a minute. Things take a slight turn for the worst for me, not a great deal, but all things change, it's the nature of everything.

Where was I? Oh yes, at our favourite restaurant, which incidentally is Italian. The restaurant is set just outside the centre of Wolverhampton and is a family run place. The people who run and wait the tables have been the same for as long as I have known. The old Italian woman who owns the place still attends the tables, she's overweight with a head full of black hair, and speaks English perfectly, but with a hint of the Italian accent.

You can call me boring if you like, but I don't even have to look at the menu when I go there. I usually have a minestrone soup to start with, followed by a lasagne Bolognese and perhaps a dessert if I'm hungry enough.

The food is beautiful, pretty much like my company.

It's strange, no matter how long we spend together Mel and I never seem to dry up on conversation, we always find something to talk about. Sometimes the subject is obscure and completely irrational, but we seem to think in the same way as each other. Saying that though, there are times when we can sit in a completely comfortable silence, times when words are not needed.

So after a night of candlelight and conversation, we head back to mine to spend the night in each other's arms.

As I'm driving home I put the radio on and we sing along together to 'I've got you babe.' The Sonny and Cher classic. I've said it before, but on the hour or every half hour afterwards things seem to happen, today it was on the hour.

After the song the radio switched to the eleven o'clock news. It told how the body of the man who had believed to have died of a heart attack with his dog had undergone a post mortem. It stated that police were now treating the death as suspicious as pieces of woollen glove found on the teeth of the dead man. It also appeared that contusions in the throat led them to believe that something had been in the throat which had caused suffocation.

Did I bolt upright and take notice of the news, I can't be entirely sure, but Mel looked at me and asked what was wrong straight away. It can be a problem being around someone who can read your every nuance, it's very hard to hide something from them when you are surprised.

The moment passed and I carried on as if nothing was wrong, Mel didn't seem too unduly concerned.

I drove home, but nagging at the back of my mind was the fact that the police were now looking more closely at this body. I knew exactly what they were going to find, if you don't guess what it is, I'll tell you what I mean later.

I tried to sing along to another song on the way, but to be honest my mind was elsewhere and I missed so many words Mel gave up singing the other half.

Have you ever driven home when you're tired from a hard day at work? I'm sure you have, a bit of a silly question really. The thing that I want to point out is the fact that despite getting home on these occasions, you can't actually remember the entire journey. You know the route so well that you almost drive on autopilot, there are twists, turns or roundabouts that you can't ever remember getting to, but you're home safe all the same. Well, this was one of those times, I was pulling up outside my house before I realised and the ignition was off in an instant. Mel gave me a sideward glance, for just a fraction of a second, but then released her seatbelt and got out of the car.

As I walked to the front door, which Mel was opening, I took hold of myself from the inside. I had just had a perfect night with Melissa, and there was no way, that news report was going to ruin everything. I gave myself a mental slap for being so stupid, put a smile on my face, and as Mel was trying to get the key into the lock (with a lot more precision than I had done after the night I had met her), I took hold of her around the waist, pulled her gently towards me and kissed her on the neck. She moved her head to one side to hold my head between her own and her shoulder. She had a wonderful natural smell that mingled to perfection with the perfume she was wearing. Heaven.

She managed to unlock and open the door; I followed her inside still holding her by the waist, and closed the front door with my right foot. She backed into me, and I held her close, I kissed her neck, which she now threw open to me, to expose as much of her neck as possible. I brushed her long blonde hair away from her ear and gently kissed every inch of the left side of her neck, from the base of ear, to just above her shoulder.

I'm not going to tell you what happened next, I'll leave that to your imagination, isn't that what these things are all about? Anyway, that kind of thing is personal, between Mel and I, and I'm sorry, on occasions like this, three is a crowd.

FOURTEEN

Perhaps now I need to explain how things turn out with this murder.

I'm not going to go back and explain in any further detail what happened between Mel and I, so don't even think about asking.

Do you know what's coming? I expect you do, unless you haven't been reading very closely. The police now confirmed that they believed that the guy I killed was not due to misadventure, as originally thought, but was murder.

Let's face it, the contusions in the throat, the wool on the teeth, and heaven forbid, my struggling, sweating DNA all over it. I'm no mathematician; in fact it took me three attempts to pass GCSE Maths, but it's easy to work out that the DNA found on the guy in Rough Wood is very similar if not exactly the same to that found on Emma Jackson.

That's almost the good thing about DNA, its not yet really an exact science, you can't really say that the two DNA samples are from the same person, simply due to the complex nature of DNA, it is completely and utterly an individual structure, each person has a unique build up of DNA; That being the case, we are still incredibly similar, not only to each other but to other mammals and even other forms of life; Hell, in terms of DNA, as the human race, we are 99.9% broccoli. This means all of the things that make us who we are, the colour of our eyes, our height, weight, skin tone, hair colour and type, the facial features that define us and the way we think are all a result of 0.01% of our DNA structure.

That being the case, it is very difficult to tell one individual from another under a microscope, unfortunately scientific advances are proving more and more successful.

All the same, I didn't really want this murder now to become a proper investigation, having almost stumbled on the heart attack story, I was reluctant to let it go.

It took quite a time before there was even a sniff of a link between the two murders, I'm not talking about days or weeks but it must have been a couple of months, and when it came it was just a mentioned after thought on the news, nothing spectacular.

Whether the police knew much before then I don't know, but if they did it certainly wasn't released to the media. Right at this point though, there's no mention of all this, and after an initial change of tack from a death by misadventure viewpoint to a murder investigation, nothing else came to light.

As I had planned, I kept myself away from the majority of media reports and developments over the following days, and to this day I don't know the guy's name.

Suffice to say that all that appeared as far as I'm aware is the fact that the police now considered the death a murder and that they had found evidence of a struggle and woollen fibres on his teeth, again they provided a 'hotline' number for any information and asked for any witnesses to come forward.

You guessed it, I didn't come forward and reveal myself as the murderer, or even that I knew anything about what had happened, like I've said before and will say time and time again, I'm not an idiot.

Life continued for me much easier after this murder than that of Emma Jackson, I didn't need to repair my car, and the stun gun was safely hidden in the loft inside a hot water bottle holder. I'm very precarious when it comes to things like that, I very rarely throw anything away that I think may become useful in the future, and that stun gun sure might come in handy.

So to put things in perspective, my job, although mind numbingly boring kept the roof over my head, the mortgage paid and even gave me a little bit of savings for those unexpected moments. Mel was perfect and I don't need to say anything else about her, I have never felt as comfortable with anyone. My friends were all happy and I was enjoying a great social life, it appeared that all the things I had hoped for, especially those with Mel, had worked out just fine, and I was now ready to move forward without the near constant head ache of Emma Jackson.

By the time all of this was settled and I only had the odd glimpse of the guy or Emma, I'd worked through the majority of spring and summer was soon to be upon us. Now during this particular summer a chain of events took place which led to an entirely untapped source for murder, well, untapped for me.

I'm getting ahead of myself a little, I supposed you hope that that was it, and that I should now say that I went on to live happily ever after and grew old and grey with Melissa, or that the police put it all together and eventually tracked me down and incarcerated me. Well neither of those two things happen, my life has been a roller coaster of events, unfortunately I'd gladly swap those lower times for those of someone else. That said, I wouldn't swap those high points that I spend with Mel for anything, they are far too precious.

FIFTEEN

I think I've said before, I've got a close bunch of friends, who are a mixture of single and couples, and we've stuck by each other, through thick and thin for years.

Mouse, is a beast of a man, 6'2" tall, a rugby player, a sportsman and probably one of the gentlest people I know. Hell, by looking at him, you certainly wouldn't want to disagree with him, he has his hair shaved close to his skull, he was broad and looked powerful, a gentle giant.

There's Chris, who you already know all about, and another key player is Mark, he's as thin and tall as me, and we share similar personalities, again though I don't think Mark has every killed anyone being one of our only differences. Oh, he's got blonde hair in comparison to my dark, its only a small difference though.

There are a few more of my friends than these three, and I may come back and go through more of them later, if it comes to it and I need to mention them, but for the time being, these three will do.

It had probably been five years since I'd been on holiday, but one Saturday afternoon, Chris and Mouse turned up at my house with brochures for holidays abroad. Summer was fast approaching and was told that wee needed to be quick if we were going to sort something out for the same year.

Apparently they had already been and spoken to a travel agent at the Co-Op and Magaluf was very popular. Personally I'd never heard of the place, and I wasn't too sure about it, not having been abroad too many times.

Malia, I'd never heard of that either, apparently it was on the island of Crete and by the look of the place in the brochure it looked fantastic, it had clear blue seas, and the climate was perfect. According to Tracey though, our very pretty and work

51

thrifty travel agent at the Co-Op, Malia was a little more expensive than Magaluf. I much preferred the look of Malia though and after a brief discussion the times, date and hotel was set and booked. Mark had agreed to everything over the telephone, he always had more money and time than the rest of us. I now needed to break into some of those savings for something somewhat less than murder. A slight annoyance.

One of the great things about my relationship with Mel is that we understand each other fully, she understands that I need time to see friends every now and then, and I understand the same from her. Don't get me wrong, neither of us exclude the other from anything, well, I don't tell her about murder, but I'm honest about everything else. Saying that I think we strike the perfect balance, we don't spend all our time in each other's pockets and have a healthy life away from each other, but we still include each other in those other aspects. When I told Mel about the holiday she was pleased to see me getting to spend some quality time with Chris, Mark and Mouse, in fact she told me she had been talking about going on holiday with her friends and a week or so later had booked one herself.

Now don't take that as a jealous or spiteful act on behalf of Mel or myself, there's not a spiteful bone in her body. We get to spend enough time (hurtful thought) together, and manage to get away on holiday together ourselves, just the two of us, in years to come. Perhaps more about that later.

The Co-Op had accepted a deposit from each of us and taken all our details, we were given a deadline when the rest of the money for the holiday needed to be paid which was fine by me, not all of my savings would be frittered away.

Another quick word, which as you will see as time goes by that impacts on me massively. Emptiness. I know right now you can't understand what I mean, but believe me, by the end you will.

At the moment though I want to reiterate that things are perfect with Mel and I, work is boring, and I've got a holiday to look forward to with Chris, Mouse and Mark. The only other part of my life that I haven't really spoken about is my family, my brother, mom and dad.

Scott still lived with mom and dad and although staying at my house every now and then, he spent most of his time flitting between mom and dad's house and his girlfriend's. Scott was at university studying to be a dentist. Of all the things he wanted to be a dentist had to be the most awful prospect, along with clowns, dentists rank highly in my fear list.

Scott had excelled at school while I had muddled along, he achieved all A grades at both GCSE and A level, and was studying dentistry at Aston University, this meant he was close enough to home to stay with mom and dad. This in turn meant he could afford a car. Clever boy.

Now, he was off for the summer, university life is amazing. He always seemed to be on a half semester or summer holiday, while I was toiling at work, yet he was going to end up earning a fortune more than me.

I had a close relationship with my family though, and it took a whole lot of will to keep my murder inside when I was with them, I wanted to tell them. Sometimes I needed someone to spill what I had done to, but loving as my family are, I would never put them in the position where they had to choose a life of happiness or prison for me.

Mom and dad were as supportive as ever with anything I wanted to do, and were happy to hear I was going on holiday in a few weeks time. In fact they even arranged to get a few Euros for my wallet for when I was over there.

I mean what else can you ask for? Such a solid and happy family life, a great relationship, and friends that are loyal and honest. Well I'll try and explain the void, I can't guarantee you'll be able to associate with it, but I'll tell you all I can.

SIXTEEN

Have you ever been a smoker? How about something harder?
Ever tried cocaine or heroine? I know; I know exactly what I can
link it to, a drug that everyone has succumbed to at some point.
Alcohol.

You can squeal until you are blue in the face that you're not an
alcoholic, and you'd be right. It's a terrible disease that is such a
struggle to overcome and far more common than society would
like to believe. Never the less, I'm sure you often partake in an
alcoholic beverage or two during the weekend, and although you
may not be reliant on the alcohol, like some, you sure do miss it
if you spend a weekend without it.

Well I'm going to try and tell you that murder is similar to
alcohol, its not really an addiction, you can live your life without
it, and you can tell yourself with a variety of explanations that
justify and rationalise it, but you have a certain hankering for it
once you've experienced it. You can say that you can go out
and don't need to drink to have a good time, in just the same
way that I can say that I *HAD* to kill that guy in Rough Wood to
relieve my memory of Emma Jackson, but as you know, by
reading these pages, nothing ever overcomes my guilt or
consoles me. The coping strategies that my mind employs to
cope with what I have done are so similar to those of an
alcoholic. It's a shame that I can only see this in hindsight.

So why rationalise? Why do I need a relief and abstract
justification for the murder, well like anyone, I'm a victim of my
own emotions and feelings. Consequently I need to tell myself
that the things I do are reasonable, which involves me building
ways to fool my conscience with excuses.

So murder is like alcohol, or any other kind of addiction,
dependence is probably too strong a word to describe it, as its
not something I'd die from if I didn't get it, pretty much like the
cocaine and heroine addiction, but its something that my brain
hungers for, and when it comes to the brain, I'm at its mercy.

I'm not sure whether you can relate to this or not, this a little bit of a taboo between people, you'll know yourself whether you know what I'm talking about, but I doubt you'd tell anyone else that you have personal experience of addiction. Don't worry, I won't tell a soul.

Now that I've given you a little of a taste of what it feels like for something for you to associate with, hopefully you can see what I'm trying to say about what it feels like inside when it comes to murder. Firstly I *had* to kill Emma after the kidnapping because there was no way I could let her live without going to jail. Secondly I *had* to kill the guy in the woods to relieve myself of the guilt of Emma, see how easy it is to justify these things. Now I'm sure you can't fully take hold of the murder concept, but at least it gives a twig of understanding.

Despite everything, there's a little bit of a niggle at the back of my mind about murder, taking someone else's life, emotions, needs, expectations is something that you will never relate to, hopefully.

As with a lot of things a little niggle can develop, like a crack in a windscreen, it can grow, and soon it becomes so large that you can't see anything else, this is what murder is like.

Another key word, succumb.

I'm an intelligent man, maybe not a well learned and studied as Scott, but intelligent all the same. Never the less, I can control many of the things I think about, even murder, to a degree, but sometimes things overwhelm me. Sometimes I get down in the doldrums, not entirely happy with my earning potential, wanting to drive a smoother luxury car in comparison to my MR2, and wondering whether I will ever be a dad, these feelings are transitory though, and within a few hours they are gone.

With murder however rather than dwindling into a mass of emotion, it seemed to have more of a substance and would often bring itself to the surface. It wasn't always in the way of killing,

I wasn't really hankering after killing someone, but more so the power that I felt when I was doing it.

I have to say the thought of all the blood, or the actual grass roots of the death are by no means appealing, it's not something I really want to do. Bludgeoning Emma was such a harsh thing to do, and it is woeful that I felt I had to do it, but it was a necessity.

Despite my intelligence and will, a little niggle can soon turn into a common thought, I'm not saying that this happens right away, or even very quickly. There's no exact amount of time between the beginning thought and the practical murder, and the time between has always been different. I just wanted to let you know that the thought was still there.

At this point though, I'm not really aware of the little niggle, I'm just going about my daily business, and the business of the day is holiday shopping. I need a pair of shorts and sunglasses.

SEVENTEEN

The Greek sun is punishing, especially when you're as pasty and light skinned as I am, the heat is like a shroud that is all enveloping, the shade is hot, inside is hot, the water is hot, everywhere is hot. Even at night.

I know I've jumped forward quite a way, but I'm sure you don't want to hear about where I bought my shorts or how much they cost and what colour they are...boring. So I thought I'd just say, all was well, and the three weeks flew by to the holiday. Everything was still great with the family, Mel was still perfect and my job was still boring. There we go, completely up to speed. I did acquire a few more items of clothing too.

It didn't really occur to me until I was sitting in the departure lounge, that I was about to be in a country nearly a thousand miles away, surely if I was to commit a murder whilst in another country like Crete, then it would be best part impossible to trace back to England. I know, that niggle the back of my mind is satiated at the moment, but it's a thought.

Like I said, as soon as the plane landed I noticed it. Everything is hot.

So, Chris, Mark, Mouse and I are sunning ourselves in the relentlessly hot Crete sun, Mouse has a strict regime to acquire an all round tan, where as I spend most of my time sheltering and trying to protect my quickly burning skin.

The sea is gorgeous though.

During the day we go to the beach, have a snorkel around the shallow part of the sea and even throw a Frisbee between each other, the normal things that young guys do on the beach. Luckily for me we didn't have a football, otherwise other beach users would have been in danger due to my lack of coordination and skill.

Despite me taking considerable care to try and protect my skin from burning, I found that my forehead was catching more than the average amount of sun and was becoming a little red, something that didn't look entirely appealing I'm sure.

On our first night at Crete we all went out to the variety of Malia nightclubs, we obviously had no idea where we were going and were dragged into practically every club along the main stretch with offers of free drinks from the beautiful women paid to get people into the bars. Suffice to say that by around 11.00 pm we were all incredibly drunk and very worse for wear. As a matter of fate there was an electrical short circuit on that first night, which closed all the bars, no lights or music. Realistically this was a blessing in disguise, as we were all on our way to serious alcohol poisoning.

We made our way back to our hotel and went off to sleep, despite the continuous punishing heat, I had no trouble getting off to sleep due to my level of drunkenness. Morning was a just a blink away, and I was soon awake with a headache after a dreamless sleep.

I was immediately hit by the heat. I looked around the room to find that everyone else was still snoring, I popped to the toilet and by the time I was done Mouse had stirred and we started talking about the previous night. We decided to take our conversation out to by the pool and leave everyone else asleep.

Being of a fairly pale nature, the sun isn't really my ideal match, it sort of burns me, makes me peel, then leaves me white. Still, I was by the pool 'catching some rays'. I was only out around 20 minutes before I started to feel the prickle that the heat was having on my skin.

I decided a dip in the pool was in order, and confidently splashed into the liquid. The confidence was soon ripped from me as my super-heated skin met the coldness of the pool and I gave a girly shriek. How manly.

After a few moments of being in the water though I was

accustomed to it, and it actually felt warm, weird. Anyway, I had a quick swim, nothing athletic, and after a few minutes dragged myself out. I gave myself a dab with the towel which was unnecessary as the heat soon dried both me and my shorts.

Mouse and I had a good chat about life and love before heading back into the apartment, by the time we got in, everyone was awake and waiting to use the shower which Chris had monopoly of.

There's another quirky thing about Greece, and that's the toilet situation. Apparently the ancient Greeks didn't take into account toilet paper, consequently this can't be flushed away. This kind of behaviour is a terrible breach of toilet etiquette for us Brits, used toilet paper in a bin just isn't cricket.

This means that as a group of four lads we needed a fast course of action that would alleviate any of us being caught in a situation that would leave us gasping for breath while we shaved or any other bathroom activity. The answer was simple.

A strict shit shower policy.

This meant that if you were going to deal dirt to the toilet it had to be followed by a liberal application of shower gel and shampoo to relieve the place of the smell, this guaranteed (almost) the next user of the bathroom to be comfortable in its use.

The days pretty much set into a routine early, we'd get up, and either sit by the pool for a while, or take a short stroll to the beach. I know what you're thinking, come on, for goodness sake, get to something more interesting. If you want to skip forward, you can, but I feel I need to tell you how I get to commit murders other than locally. So, for the patient ones, I'll continue.

Chris and I would often stop off from the beach and take in an ice cold glass of beer, or two. So that the beer is incredibly cold, not only do they chill the beer, but in Crete they also freeze the

59

glass. Ok, there's a lot of dripping from the condensation, but it sure does stay chilled.

Like I've said, right now, I'm not really aware of any niggles at the back of my mind. Of course, I'm missing Melissa, and the guy from the woods slips into my thoughts or a dream, just like Emma Jackson, but really I've managed on the whole to put these things behind me. I am enjoying being in Crete.

It is not during the day though that is important, it on the evening, when we've all had our fill of a hearty meal, and head into the town to dance and drink. That's when something important happens, but just as always, none of us know it yet.

I think it was out third night out in Crete, we were in a club, myself, Mouse, Chris and Mark are out in nightclub when Chris gets approached by a girl who had been dancing at the opposite side of the dance floor from us. Her friend approaches Mark and before I know it me and Mouse are dancing together like a gay couple.

Funnily enough, no girls approach us.

Mouse and I finally get the picture, and decide to leave Chris and Mark alone with the girls and we find a different club, and keep up the heavy regime of drinking. The great thing about Malia is that you can get half cut simply by walking from club to club. There are people paid to stand outside each and every club offering free drinks to customers who will go inside. Call me cheap, but Mouse and I visited more than a few clubs and had our fair share of freebies.

It was a bit of a weird night, and I didn't see Chris again until the following morning. That being the case, he had managed to get back to the hotel where we were staying, and even into the apartment without me noticing, I was so deeply unconscious from my intoxicated sleep.

It was around 10 o-clock that I got up, went for a shower, and by the time I got out of the shower, Mouse was up and we decided to go and sit by the pool.

Chris came down to the pool a couple of hours later to tell us that he was going to spend the day with the girl that he had met last night. I told to him to enjoy the day and to behave, he gave me a wry smile as he walked back to the apartment.

Mouse and I spent a lot of the day recovering by the pool from last night, while Mouse lapped up the sun's rays, I hid beneath a towel and read a book, the sun had already burned me, and I didn't fancy sunstroke.

I spent a lot of time with Mouse over the course of the week, on our fifth day, Chris said an emotional goodbye to the girl he met on our second night, as she was returning home.

The last couple of days flew by and before I knew it, I was packing my case for our flight back home, Chris had already said that he was going to see the girl again when he got back home. I found out that her name was Clara, and she lived in Glasgow.

Do you see where I'm going now? I expect so. The holiday turns out to be much more than a simple summer fling for Chris and Clara, which becomes so much more important for me in the future.

The flight back home was initially delayed for a couple of hours and we sat in the airport sweating, Heraklion airport is not the most comfortable place to be stranded for hours on end due to delays. Luckily the delay was only those couple of hours, and we were soon taking our last few gulps of warm Crete air as we strode along the airport tarmac and to the plane.

Like any economy class flight, the standard isn't great on the plane, being nearly six feet tall my legs barely fit in the gap; Mouse is having a real struggle. A journey of nearly 4 hours in cramped conditions doesn't do much for your circulation; luckily they gave me some exercises to do.

Despite a slight bout of turbulence that made a couple of passengers on board give out a stifled yelp, the journey was uninteresting. I can't remember what film was playing, but because I didn't buy a pair of headphones from the cabin crew, I couldn't hear it anyway.

I think Chris spent a lot of time talking to Mark about their romances, I was looking forward to getting home and seeing Mel. By the time the plane had landed Chris and Mark had already devised a plan of when they'd be travelling up to Glasgow to rekindle everything with the girls. I thought it was a little premature, wondering whether the girls would even answer a call off them in the 'real world'.

We had made arrangements with our families to pick us up from Birmingham Airport, and as I came through the exit gate I saw my mom and dad waiting for me. I gave them a hug and kiss and talked about the holiday as we walked towards the car park.

They told me that my tan gave me a healthy look, whatever that means. I'm more than happy with being pallid.

On the ride back to my house, I decided to close my eyes for a while, which was usually the way when I'm a passenger in a car, I find it difficult to stay awake. Besides, the enclosed and pressurised aircraft had given me a slight ache the back of my eyes, a kind of hangover headache. You know what I mean.

When I got back to mine, I was exhausted. Still I made mom and dad a cup of coffee with the bottle of milk mom had bought with her for me. Mom was always so thoughtful about things like that. We talked about how everyone had been while I was away, and what they had been up to, and after an hour or so, they left so that I could unpack; that will wait till morning I thought, and went straight off to bed.

EIGHTEEN

Remember that little niggle I told you about? Well, this starts to come into play about now. The splinter embedded in the back of my mind starts to fester and grow, and what it festers and grows into is my next victim.

At the back of my mind, somewhere deep, so as it didn't start encroaching on my daily life, was the thought that the police may be tracing me. I hadn't heard anything about the guy in the woods or Emma for quite a while, which made me think one of three things.

Either, a) they had come to no conclusions, drawn no lines of further enquiry and were waiting for a lead from somewhere else. b) Connected the two murders, despite being on different forces, but were unable to link either to an offender, or c) were hot on my tracks and were just waiting for the right time to knock down the door and take me into custody.

There are times when the rational side of the brain remains in control, let's face it, if they were going to try and arrest me, and they knew it was me, then they wouldn't be hanging around, I would be awaiting sentencing by now.

There are other times though when the not so rational part of the brain takes control, as you no doubt have already noticed. This is when I start thinking that I'm hours away from capture, this is when the niggle develops.

'I mean, what if I am just hours away from capture? There is still so much more inside me, I'd feel wasted. There is still so much more that I need/want to do, I don't want to go down with only two murders under my belt.'

It may be hard for you to conceive, but that was how I was thinking.

There's also something that you probably won't realise, again it involves the internet, and will no doubt surprise you. Whether it's a coincidence again or not, but my next murder involves a delivery from America via the internet.

Firstly I'll tell you something that you do know, and that's that the chemical Chloroform causes unconsciousness when inhaled. This next part though is probably going to surprise you.

A spray widely used in America for starting car engines in the winter contains a chemical called Ether. This helps engines start due to its very quick evaporation rate. Ether though has a very similar effect to Chloroform when inhaled and replaced Chloroform for used in medicine some time ago.

You've probably guessed what's coming, a ten dollar purchase for Auto Start, from an auto parts website and I'm well in my way to my next murder.

It surprises me how cheap this is, its a good job I opened that saving account after the first murder, there's going to be plenty of spare money again.

Again my foremost thought was to evade capture, and despite Rough Wood being an ideal place, I didn't want to arouse suspicion any more than had been aroused already. So in needed to find a more secluded and unusual location.

From any good book store, get yourself a copy of walks in the midlands. You'll find a nice little place called Great Whitley and Abberley Hills, which is a decent 6 mile walk around Whitley Court and the surrounding countryside.

I'm not going to get into any boring detail about the in betweens, but Christmas was fantastic with Mel, and if a relationship can get any better, and believe me, each day I think it can't, and that we are at the peak of what a relationship can be. Yet it does.

What's best is that I return to the Abberley Hills, a great place for a sunny day walk for those who like the outdoors, or even just to keep fit, even better for an Autumn murder.

NINETEEN

So, it's January and like I said, Christmas was fantastic and heading into New Year was perfect, but that's not really what's important. The important part comes in early January.

It's cold. I mean, there's ice on my windscreen when I get up and go to work, I can see my own breath when I breathe and the steering wheel is freezing against my skin.

It's a Sunday though, and I'm not up as early as when I go to work, but I get up before I my ritual lie in, as I want to make sure that I get to the Abberley Hills in a good time. Mel thinks I'm going to spend the day visiting my family for a change, I haven't seen my mom and dad for a while.

It's not as much of a drive from Wednesbury as I thought, and within an hour I'm parked up on the car park outside a community centre. I put my walking boots on, take hold of my 'Pathfinder' Midlands Walks book, and head off into the hills.

Now what I was after was someone just like the guy I killed in Rough Wood, no-one around and him not found for some time.

As you kind of guess, as with anything, things don't go exactly to plan. Never the less, I don't know the outcome yet, and head off, checking everything I need is in my pockets.

For the first half a mile or so I'm on roads, and as I eventually head into the hills I take another look at the map to make sure I'm on the right track. I wished at that moment that Mel was with me, she was always reassuring. On the other hand, I doubt she would want to be with me any longer if she was with me for what I was planning to do.

I've got to say, if you are ever planning to go walking, and want to stay fairly mud free, then don't take the Abberley Hills in January. The first hill you come to is a nightmare. It seems to be un-ending, and in January is as immensely slippery. I found myself clawing at leafless bushes and trees trying to haul myself up the hill.

Having reached towards the top of the hill though is where everything becomes interesting.

There's a little recess before the pinnacle of the ridge, and this is where she was. She was around 40 years old and of slight build. She was wearing all of the walking gear you could imagine. She even had a small stick, to help with difficult climbs.

As I approached her, I gave a little smile. In my pocket I flicked off the top of the Auto Start can. With the top off the can there wasn't a lot of room in my pocket, and I started to fumble. What this must have looked like to the woman I don't know. Fear spread quickly across her face as I approached, despite my smile. Then I realised. I'm half way up a deserted hill smiling at a woman while rummaging around in my pockets. She must have thought I was about to get my knob out or something.

I decided that I was going to go all out this time. Unfortunately, the ground was slippery beneath my foot as I started to lunge towards her, I lost my footing. I made a quick lunge towards her, but despite this being a surprise, my foot slipping away from me made my action all too telegraphed. Her suspicion of my pocket fumbling made her quickly start to run away.

I'm a lot younger than her, and a lot lighter on my feet, so luckily I'm quickly upon her, but my heart is in my throat and pounding. I grabbed her around the neck. I put my entire arm around her throat so that she was held under my right armpit by her neck. Her cheek was pressed hard against my ribs.

This gave me some use of my right hand and I placed the can of Auto Star in it and held the handkerchief in my left hand. I sprayed the Auto Start onto the handkerchief and dropped the can. Although she was struggling, I had far superior strength. Luckily there was no dog to contend with as well.

I held the handkerchief against her mouth and nose, until within a minute or less she was limp. I indignantly dropped her to the ground and she lay with her face in the mud. For some reason, and I don't know why, perhaps just because I could, I stamped on the back of her head, crushing her face against the ground. I felt something crack under foot. I don't know what it was.

I took the shoe lace from my pocket and stretched it to its fullest. I grabbed her by he hair and pulled her face from the mud, blood dripped from her nose as I lifted it.

The Ether was working well though.

I pulled the shoe lace over her head so that it rested on her throat. I let her head go and it slapped hard back into the mud.

I took hold of each end of the shoe lace and made sure that it was in position on her throat, I placed my knee on the back of her head, so that my right leg trailed down her neck and my foot nestled in the middle of her back. I wrapped the shoelace around the middle and forefinger on each hand and pulled both ends of the shoe lace with all of my strength. The lace cut into my fingers, right where they meet the main part of my hand.

I quickly look up and saw that the view across Worcester was brilliant, if not a little covered by the low cloud.

I turned my attention back to her and could see the lace digging in deeply to her throat, despite the Ether making her unconscious she was still breathing, well, only for about 30 seconds, until the shoe lace cut off everything to her brain. There was no struggling this time, I wasn't sweating and this was comparatively easy, especially after the last one. If she pissed herself, I couldn't see it in the already dark earth.

Once she was dead, I decided I wasn't going to bother trying to cover my tracks, lets face it, they'd already come to the murder conclusion on both of my previous accounts, despite me trying to make it seem otherwise. So I left the shoelace around her neck, picked up the can of Auto Start, and headed towards the peak of the hills.

At the very summit, where the ridge of the hills reaches their highest, there's a large white triangulation point, this particular one was purchased and maintained by the Bourneville Trust. Birmingham having its own little say on Worcestershire's Abberley Hills.

It took me best part of 2 hours to get myself back to the car, by sticking to the paths. When I got there I was disgusted with myself, my jeans were covered in mud.

TWENTY

The drive home was a blur, I always seem to get like it after I kill someone. I know that there was nothing wrong with my driving, despite being on autopilot, but I can barely remember the way back. Not once though was I staring into oblivion when approaching an island or traffic lights, having to slam on the brakes or anything, its just my driving was more autonomic than thought about.

I pulled up outside my house and got out of the car, the first thing I noticed was that I had got mud all over the seats of the MR2, I sighed at the thought at having to spend more money getting the seats upholstered.

I went inside and made a cup of tea, the first thing I ever do when I get home.

As usual the tea remained un-drunk as the television blared away in the corner while I sat on the sofa in a semi-trance. It was the telephone ringing that bought me out of the trance. I recognised the number on the display of the phone straight away. Mel.

I sat and talked with Mel for best part of an hour, our conversation never once stifled, and to be honest I don't know how we filled almost an entire hour of non-stop conversation, but not once did we sit in silence.

We made plans to meet up later in the week, and if I'm honest, I'm glad I wasn't going to be meeting her later that day, I felt empty and wasn't quite altogether me. I needed some time to recover from what I had done today. After the phone call I fell off to sleep, the fire blazing and the television blaring, my head resting on the back of the sofa, my throat exposed to the ceiling.

I don't really know how long I was asleep, because I don't know what time I dropped off. I know it was approaching two in the morning though because I remember looking at the clock. I stood up and stretched, my neck was a little sore from the awkward position I had been in, and I almost knocked the cup of tea over that I had placed on the floor at some point before I fell asleep.

I turned off the television, the fire and the lights that I'd left on and headed upstairs to bed.

I'd like to say that I had a heavy and happy sleep, but I didn't, it was restless and I was fidgeting all night. It wasn't just the dreams that were making me restless, and don't ask me to tell you what they were so that you can analyse them, because I can't remember them, but I had a terrible headache.

It was around four o'clock that I had to get up and take a couple of Ibuprofen tablets.

I watched the news channel for around half an hour before heading back off to bed, this time after an initial period of fidgeting and trying to make myself comfortable, I fell off to sleep, it was nearly midday before I awoke.

With it being nearly midday was not particularly a good thing, especially as I was meant to be at work. I had three missed calls on my mobile phone, I never gave out my home number to work or colleagues, and realised that I had to call in to make my apologies and give an excuse.

After only a few minutes of talking to my boss with a croaky voice, she was convinced that bed was the best place for me for the next couple of days. I sure could put on that ill voice when I needed to.

As a matter of fact the next couple of days free from work would be ideal to get over what I had done. I know that this isn't the first time, and I imagine that you're wondering what I'm still doing acting like this after I kill someone. Let's face it, all the movies you've seen tell you that as soon as someone has the 'thirst' for murder, they love every next one.

That's not me.

71

The difference between Hollywood and reality is harsh, and I have never had a thirst, or enjoyed what I have done, nor have I ever felt a release after I have killed someone. It has never been for vengeance and if I could go back and change that first moment with Emma Jackson I would do. I'm not proud of it and I don't exaggerate, boast or regale stories to people with what I have done. In fact, as you know I have to try and forget and overcome these murders every single time.

Isn't life such a hardship for me!

Well, I have the next couple of days off work and by the time I go back I make sure that I've got a pocket full of disposable handkerchiefs, it all helps in the illness façade.

By the time Thursday comes I get to see Mel, I pick her up after work, and after briefly stopping off at her parents house, we carry on to mine. We've picked out a DVD to watch and picked up a bottle of wine from the Asda supermarket, which lies around a mile away from my house.

We spend the evening in each other's arms, in front of the fire watching the DVD. We talk throughout the film and it the quality kind of talk. We talk of life, religion, aliens, ghosts and death. When it comes to talking of death I become fairly uneasy. Like I said a while back, the jury is still out for me, and I'm not sure what to expect when the big moment comes.

When I get into work on Friday the car park is fairly empty and I realise that I'm earlier than normal, by the time Jane gets into the office, my computer is warm and I've already completed a fair amount of work.

Jane sits at her desk, and despite everything I look at her legs. I don't know what it is about me, I mean Mel is awesome and if I had to look at either Jane's legs or Mel's, it would be Mel's every time, but that doesn't stop me looking.

Jane catches me taking a glimpse, and moves her skirt to cover her thigh that I could see, and I feel somewhat embarrassed that I have been busted looking at her legs.

I give myself an internal curse and get back to work.

I can't tell you how boring my work is. Pensions and life assurance aren't the life and soul of any party at the best of times, so to be trying to work after the exhilaration and adrenaline filled moments during killing someone, makes the monotony of normal day sound like life, but with the volume turned down.

Half way through the day I was starting to feel tired, and decided I'd have the afternoon off, I told my boss she could either take it from my annual leave, or I'd make it up during the flexi-hours the following week. Either way, I was off home after lunch on Friday.

.

TWENTY ONE

It was funny, but I didn't hear anything about number three at all. By that I don't mean I kept myself away from the media or anything, but I just didn't hear anything.

Let's face it, it was clear it was a murder, the shoelace was still tightly around her neck, this was no shoe tying accident. She was in the middle of a popular woodland walk, I know it was little way away, but the news programs tell me about murders in Bradford let alone just up the road in Worcester.

I don't know whether the lack of any news was unnerving me, or whether there was a morbid curiosity about the woman, but I wasn't comfortable with nothing at all.

Isn't this what they say? A murderer always returns to the scene of the crime? Well, I'm not you're normal murderer, and there was no way I was going to go anywhere near those hills for the rest of my life. I was interested though as to why nothing had surfaced about her.

There was only one answer, the internet. The internet is the most lurid and abundant source of information regarding any subject, accessible at any time. The first place I looked gave me the surprising answer I was after. I logged onto the Warwickshire Gazette, a local newspaper for local people, tackling local issues.

Luckily there was an archive section of the internet site and I was able to look at back issues of the newspaper. I went back three months, to the day that I killed the woman and started a trawl through the paper looking for any kind of clue.

Although interested I wasn't obsessed, and there was no way I was going to pick my way through the entire paper as if back at university looking for any kind of quote on the subject I was discussing in an essay. No, if it didn't come in big bold letters, I wasn't interested.

I say that, but when there was nothing in big bold letters, I decided to have a deeper look. I came across her about half an hour into the search.

I talk about coincidence all the time, how about irony? Do I talk about that? Well, isn't it ironic that the one person that I kill, that I decide not to try and hide ends up being a missing person.

I really don't know what happened to her body, because I made no attempt to hide it at all, yet here I am, sitting in front of the computer at my mom and dad's house reading about a woman who had gone missing. I recognised her face.

Apparently members of her family had placed posters around the Abberley Hills, which was where they knew she was headed when she left the house.

Now somewhere on those hills was her body, with a shoelace wrapped tightly around the throat, and I was sitting in awe that it hadn't been discovered. I may have been somewhat relieved that it hadn't been discovered, but more so surprised.

Obviously I made no attempt to alert anyone that the body was somewhere amongst the hills, especially as when they did come across it they would see that it had been killed, not just died, and then would come the difficult questions. Oh, no, I'm keeping quiet.

I started to wonder what was better for those left. The question of what had happened to them or whether they would see their loved one again; or the knowledge that it was over and that one special person was lost forever more, and that that person had been stolen from them by someone else.

I don't know the answer, but for me, the emotion displayed by Emma Jackson's parents on TV were more than enough to show me that the knowledge of murder was a tragic emotion, but then perhaps I'm not the best person to judge this kind of thing. I have purely self-motivated reasons.

75

A harsh thought I know, but this type of thinking was keeping that niggle at bay. This was a good thing for me, as I needed time to get over this murder and spending time with Mel was part of the answer.

So, there's a body in the hills that no-one is aware of but me. OK, the family might be contemplating their worst fears, but really, I was the only one who knew.

It may seem strange, but the reassurance that the police were not breathing down my neck over this murder made it all the easier to overcome. I didn't have to cover anything, up and despite not trying to hide the murder, it had somehow worked out in my favour.

I'm not saying that it was easy to get over, just easier than the last two. I know just what I needed, a night at the old Italian restaurant with Mel.

TWENTY TWO

Have you ever heard the saying 'you can't see the woods for the trees'? I know its something I've heard quite often, but as Mel and I were sitting in the Italian restaurant, I had a true glimpse of the woods.

Mel and I had been spending more and more time with each other, and more often than not these days, she was staying at my house. There were toiletries in the bathroom and a whole lot of wardrobe dedicated to her. This wasn't something that had been planned and talked about, it was just something that had happened over time.

It was when I was taking a sip from a spoonful of minestrone soup that I looked up and saw her. I was looking at her as if I'd never seen her before. As if she were the night stars, and I was a child, in awe at the magnificent view. I don't think she noticed, and moments are simply that and pass in a blink. If I close my eyes I can see her, right there, right then.

She wasn't doing anything provocative, she wasn't licking her lips in enjoyment of her own food, or anything like that, she was just sitting opposite me. As soon as my spoon was empty I knew, my mind had realised what my heart had known. I loved her, and she was the person I wanted to share my life with.

Now I don't think sharing everything about my life would progress our relationship much, women seem to shrink away from pathological killer types. Or so I've heard.

Obviously though I didn't just stand up at the table and shout it out for all and sundry to hear. I'm sure Mel would have been a little embarrassed and shocked, so I just sat there, content with my own thoughts. I wanted to tell her though, and felt it welling up inside of me, almost bursting from my throat without any consideration for anything. I held onto to it, and we finished our meals with pure and simple conversation on daily events.

With this new realisation came a couple things, firstly I found that whenever I was with her I kept taking sly glances at her while she wasn't noticing. Nothing special just if she was watching TV I'd look at her and sit and enjoy her profile for a while, she would inevitably catch me, as I'm sure people can tell when you are looking at them, even if they can't see you.

Secondly I found that I wasn't thinking about the murders I had committed and that little niggle was completely absent. I don't mean that some of the effects like struggling to get off to sleep, or finding myself thinking about while I'm on the toilet are reduced, I mean that I wasn't thinking of it at all. A Huey Lewis and the News song comes to mind "That's the power of love."

During the drive home I kept making those side wards glances I was telling you about, keeping my head facing forwards. Sometimes I'd look and she'd already be looking at me driving.

We pulled up outside my house and went inside, I offered to make us a cup of tea, but instead she took me by the hand and led me upstairs. Well, you know what happened next, but suffice to say that it was fantastic. We slept in each others arms.

I awoke to find Mel still sleeping in my arms; my left arm had pins and needles and I was just able to slide it from beneath her, via the gap of the back of her neck. She murmured but didn't wake.

I went downstairs and put some fresh coffee in the machine. I left the percolator percolating with it gargling in the corner while I went about making some scrambled eggs on toast for us. I like to put a little dash of herbs into my scrambled eggs for a little extra taste.

By the time I was finished making the coffee and the scrambled eggs I turned to find Mel standing in the kitchen doorway, wrapped in my oversized dressing gown. She looked beautiful. As with many things if I'd said to her that she looked beautiful she would have responded with words like "I've got panda eyes; my hair is a mess or I'm too pale" I don't think women truly understand how beautiful they are, without make up and especially in the morning. Despite those words that would follow I told her that she looked beautiful anyway. I don't know if she believed me or not, but it was sincere. She really was a beautiful sight to behold.

Being a Sunday afternoon we were able to lounge around the house for most of the day. I popped out as midday was nearly upon us and picked up a cooked chicken from Asda. I'd prepared the vegetables for a roast chicken lunch and by two o clock we were chowing down on the bird.

I didn't say anything to Mel about what had happened at the restaurant and what I thought and felt. I wanted to wait for a better time to tell her instead of blurting it out with a mouthful of potatoes and chicken.

TWENTY THREE

From the point that I discovered my infatuation and love for Mel, the necessity for murder seemed to fade away into insignificance. I barely thought about the people I had killed, and that niggle that sometimes seemed to creep into my mind was non existent. I know that is a harsh thing to say, to minimalise and de-grade murder, but its true, I was so involved in my own life and Mel.

Looking back on things now, I also wonder whether if things would have been different if I'd met her months before I did.

Let's face it, there is a distinct possibility that I wouldn't have been so abstract in my thoughts whilst at work, and I might never have knocked Emma Jackson down.

That wouldn't really make for an interesting story though, would it?

I have to say that the next few months seem to be a bit of blur to me, I don't think I can remember all the exact details about what happened, and to be honest the exact details don't really matter; it's the broad brush of the story that's important here, not the trivial pieces of information.

There are a few things that seemed to happen at the same sort of time, all of which are quite important.

Firstly and most obviously were my own internal feelings about Mel, although not being outwardly preoccupied, internally it was all I could think of, but more of that later.

Secondly was Chris, I know it's been a while since I've spoken about it, but its time to elaborate on Chris and Clara.

I have to say that there was a considerable amount of mockery towards Chris when he said that he was going to be seeing Clara again, and although that may sound insulting, it was the way our group of friends worked, there was a lot of healthy jesting.

Despite this, Chris took the jibe well and headed up a monthly trip to Glasgow to see Clara. This was peppered with Clara taking trips down to Wolverhampton to be with Chris. To be honest it was refreshing to have someone new in the group when we went out, and Clara fitted right into 'our gang' from the outset.

Clara had an infectious get up and go attitude and personality that rubbed off on us all when we were out, and I enjoyed seeing her having fun with us, dancing like mad to the songs at Cheeky Monkeys.

In fact it was Clara and Chris that sparked a wave of camping in the Lake District for the group. I can't tell you anything about any of that though, because camping is alien to me. If I was going on holiday I wanted it to be relaxing, not stressful and windy. I preferred a shower in my room, and a toilet right next to it, if I had wanted to 'ruff it' I would, if I wanted s site with all the amenities, I might as well get a hotel room.

So, while everyone else was camping out over at the Lake District, I was spending my time with Mel, nothing exciting, we just went to Blockbuster, which was just round the corner from my house and picked up a DVD that we both wanted to see.

Unlike most couples, there was no decision to be made between us, no compromise, as we both wanted the same film, which was the uncanny thing about us, we seemed to flow together, and even looking back now I can't remember a single disagreement. That may seem hard to believe, but it's true.

If you don't believe that it's possible to be with someone that you don't argue with, and instead believe that arguments are just a reason to make up, then leave your partner, there is someone else out there who fits you altogether better.

The film fitted us both, something scary and creepy, which made us sit incredibly close together on the sofa, while the fire blazed

81

away to our right. With the lights off and a lamp on the opposite side of the room our only light against the glare of the television, we held each other close, as if what we saw on the screen could somehow transfer itself to real life.

I don't know what point it was, but I felt it, the feeling climbed itself up from my stomach, through my chest and sat in my throat, just waiting for me to open my mouth.

The film was almost finished and the twist of an end was about to reveal itself, and I had no choice but to reveal myself. I said her name quite quietly, so that her attention was drawn to me. With the lights turned off and the lamp and television our only source of light, Mel's eyes sparkled and reflected the little amount available straight into my eyes.

I used both of my hands and swept her long blond hair behind her ears, so that the hair was pinned between her ears and her head. I did this slowly and with purpose. I could see the inquisitive look on her face.

TWENTY FOUR

Now I have to say, I missed the significance of the wedding ring rolling across the floor, and the fact that there was a table in front of the door leading to the office, and I didn't even see the significance of being able to see her breath in the cold air while he was talking to her.

I was far too obsessed with what I was about to say to the gorgeous woman sitting next to me, Mel seemed slightly annoyed that I was ruining the best part of the film. Not that either of us knew we were at the best part of the film.

Despite me interrupting the film, and although Mel had one eye trying to keep up with the action, Mel looked at me with an expression of curious wonder.

I've found that women have an uncanny instinct of knowing what men are thinking, and they know this usually well before the men know themselves. Although I had tried my hardest to keep my emotions deep within, when I looked at her there was a slight hint of a wry smile edging at the corners of her mouth. A smile that said: 'I know what's coming, but want to hear what you have to say.'

Then it came out, while I was looking at her, looking straight into those deep blue oceans for eyes, I said it, a phrase it seemed I had longed to say to her for eternity.

"I love you."

Her wry smile instantly turned into a one that occupied the most of her lower face, and her teeth were bare open to me. She flung her arms around me, instantly forgetting all about the significance that dead people sometimes don't even realise that they are dead.

Our embrace could have lasted for years, or it could have only been a few seconds, I lost complete lack of time. One of those moments, that when my own death finally comes I will linger on and cherish, to live over and over again, forever lost in the moment of happiness.

If I'm honest though, it must have only have been seconds, these moments can seem so much longer though. After the embrace Mel gave me a long hard kiss, and when we came up for air, she repeated the words to me. She looked straight into my eyes with the exact same intent that I had used to look into her eyes just moments before.

We spent the remainder of the evening in each others arms, even closer than when watching the film, by the time I came to my senses the DVD player was burning a whole through the disc, as the intro credits replayed itself over and over, and I dread to think how long it had been playing the same sequence.

I have to say at this point, in case there is any suspicion that something terrible happens to Mel at my hands, that there is no way I would do something like that. I would have moved mountains for Mel, I would have protected her from any danger, and she would have been the very last person on my list of potential murder victims.

I have found in the years that have passed, that those people who are most important to me have stuck it with me through thick and thin. I have always known that I could count on either Chris or Matt, at any time to give me either reassurance or approval.

So, Bruce has been dead for some time…. I honestly didn't realise, and to be honest, I usually see most things coming, and it's strange for me to be caught out.

Mel is looking at me, an expression on her face that makes my heart beat faster, its hard to believe but my mouth is watering, like one of Pavlov's dogs. I look into her eyes and can barely contain the love that I feel. If I was 20 stone and 7' tall I expect people would be able to understand where I fit all the emotion I felt, but at only 5'11" my emotion feels like it is bursting from within me.

84

Mel takes me by the hand and we go upstairs.

TWENTY FIVE

Again, I've said it before but three is a crowd and what goes on behind my closed bedroom door, stays there, Mel would be pretty upset if anything about what went on in there came out in these pages, and it would make me embarrassed myself.

Besides, there is more I need to tell you about, and going on about things like that is only prolonging a story that will take all of my will to tell, and if you want to know the end, then I have to leave all that stuff out.

I have to get back to Chris and Clara, as you've no doubt guessed, they have a large part to play in murder, I'm not saying that they have a hand in it or anything, well at least not a dirty blood soaked direct hand in murder. Moreover that I involve them in an indirect way.

It was after about a year and a half that Chris broke the news to the rest of us that he was looking for a job and a house up in Glasgow so that he could move in with Clara. I can't say I was surprised but it was still quite a shock to think that my best friend would be moving nearly 300 miles away.

Before long we were all gathered together in the Crown and Cushion Pub drinking a farewell drink to Chris. It was a Friday night and he had packed all of his stuff into a Ford Transit in preparation of making the drive on Sunday, lets face it after tonight he would be needing the most of Saturday to recover.

The pub was absolutely packed, but it was a great night, Chris managed to get himself incredibly drunk, well, we managed to get Chris incredibly drunk, and it was the kind of send off he wanted.

I saw Chris on the Saturday and he looked grey and dehydrated, his eyes had the appearance of a pair that had been open for most of the night with a finger poking each one, he was a mess. He didn't fancy anything to eat, and was prone to feeling sick at hearing the word Vodka, I wouldn't have dared to bring an alcoholic drink anywhere near him.

Isn't it at the most innocuous times, when we are most vulnerable, when we are relaxed when things hit us unexpectedly? Isn't it these times when those things hit us harder than at any other? Well I found it did, and I was knocked for six.

Chris invited me into the living room and I was instantly attacked by his over friendly dog, I must admit I played a bit of a part in the dog's excitement as I always made a fuss and played with him when I was at Chris' house. So it had to be expected that he was jumping up at me and bringing me his pull toy when I came.

Chris collapsed onto the sofa when he got into the living room, a bottle of Lucozade rested against the sofa on the floor, about two inches of liquid already taken in by Chris, but clearly a difficult task. The TV was blaring in the background and I was joking with Chris about how terrible he looked, when he took hold of the remote control and turned the TV up.

I turned to the TV to see a familiar scene, the Abberley Hills, and a scroll across the bottom of the screen said that a body of a woman had been found somewhere in the area, a woman who had been missing for some time.

The further bombshell was dropped that police who were called to the scene believed that it was murder and not misadventure or anything else....surprise surprise, she had a shoelace around her neck, it wouldn't take Columbo to work that she hadn't had a freak shoe tying accident.

Whether the colour drained from my face I don't know, but Chris started poking fun at me, telling me how rotten I looked all of a sudden. I asked him for a glass of Lucozade, and uncomfortably settled into the lush padded chair. I gulped the Lucozade down within a couple of moments of sitting I got up and headed to the toilet. Chris asked me if I needed a full

87

English breakfast as I left the room in a stab of satire believing my current illness to be bought on by alcohol. I fashioned a kind of grin and left.

I locked the bathroom door and sat on the seat, the seat was down but it was the support I was after, not the toilet. Sweat had developed on my forehead and I was feeling queasy.

This hadn't really happened before, I hadn't had a reaction like this before to the news that someone had been murdered; let's face it, I already knew what had happened so it shouldn't be a shock. I think it was the news that the police had discovered yet another of my murdered bodies, made me feel a little nervous.

Whether there was a link to the alcohol or not, but I did come over feeling quite sickly. I could feel the saliva glands at the side of my mouth working over time, giving me a tingling sensation in my jaw and a build up of saliva; a sensation that said 'Hold onto that gleaming white bowl with both arms, you're about to need it.' I swallowed numerous times in a bid to keep the vomit away and after about half a minute or so the feeling subsided and I escaped, vomit free.

I composed myself, looked at myself in the mirror, took a deep breath and unlocked the bathroom door. I went downstairs to where Chris lolled on the sofa, taking sips gingerly from the Lucozade bottle. He looked up when I came in.

"Feel better?" he asked "I always feel better after a good sick, give it twenty mins though and you'll be back where you were....the flood gates are open." He continued without an utterance from me.

I collapsed into the chair and watched the TV, the news had already changed to a different story, and Chris clearly hadn't paid much attention to the murder. It occupied my thoughts almost entirely.

I made my excuses to Chris and said I was going home to try and get some rest, and added that I could feel and major headache coming on and wanted to get back before it took hold.

The drive back home, as seems to be quite often when I hear bad news, was on autopilot and what seemed like no time at all I was pulling up outside my house. I opened and closed the front door, and rested against the door once it was closed. The headache I had mentioned to Chris was now in full swing and I went straight to the kitchen and found a couple of Ibuprofen tablets, I took these with a glass of cold tap water.

I made my way upstairs, taking off my t-shirt and jeans on the way, so that I was in my pants and socks when I climbed into bed. I lay in bed and tossed and turned, my headache was becoming a real blinding migraine pain, and I was feeling incredibly ill; in all honesty this was probably the result of receiving the sickening news, the alcohol the previous night and the development of my migraine.

I don't know how long it took, but eventually sleep arrived, despite it being early afternoon, and in my slumber I dreamt.

TWENTY SIX

Clair de Lune by Debussy was playing softly in my ears, I turned over leaving a patch of wet dribble on the pillow. I was frowning as my eyes opened and realised that it was mobile phone that was ringing. I leaned over to snatch the phone from the bedside cabinet, but it slipped from my grasp and landed on the floor with a bump. The call ended.

It was lucky I hadn't answered the call as I could tell that my voice would croak and I would have been disorientated.

After a couple of seconds adjusting to waking life, I picked up my phone. For the moment the murder was not even registering in my mind, and I hadn't noticed that I no longer had a headache. I clicked a couple of the buttons and saw Mel's name and number pop up in the display. I hadn't spoken to her all day, she must have been worried.

I looked at the time as displayed on my mobile phone and saw that I had been asleep a good couple of hours. I got up and went to the kitchen to help myself to a glass of water, in order to soothe my throat, as I walked through the living room I realised the living room curtains were open and I was dressed in merely my pants. I ran upstairs and grabbed my dressing gown, and taking my mobile phone downstairs with me.

I called Mel, who was a little annoyed at me for not contacting her sooner but was glad I was ok. She was out shopping with her friends and we arranged that she would come to mine later on the evening and that I would cook her meal.

Now it was this kind of thing that kept my mind active and my guilt at bay. Every now and then through the day I found myself switching off from what I was doing and thinking about the woman in the Abberley Hills. My mind was sort of caught on a single element of what happened, not the entire act, there was just one thing sticking out for me.

It was the sound, the sound of her struggling for breath and gagging. The sound of the spittle resting on her voice box, making a sort of wheezing gurgle as she tried to pass air across it, air that simply was not coming. Her body had been completely limp, so there were no nails scratching at the tort shoelace around her neck, it was just that horrific gurgling sound, as her unconscious body tried its best to breathe.

I had to see what was going on, and tuned the TV onto SKY news to see if I could hear anything about the woman from the hills.

This may sound strange, but there would perhaps on the outside seem to be more similar with this murder as with the man in Rough Wood, but inside I felt like it was closer to that of Emma Jackson. With my mind being caught on the sound made through the gurgling made me directly link the sound with the awful crack of the claw hammer against Emma's skull.

I was in a place where I had tried so hard not to be, caught up in the guilt and emotional torment of having killed those people.

I tried to bring myself into line by getting back to my life, I know that those peoples lives had been cut short by me, but in order to get over that I had to try and get back to my life. Life for me was concentrating on what I was going to do for Mel when she arrived, I decided I was going to make it a special occasion with candles and wine.

Now I can't remember exactly what the meal was, or what wine accompanied it, but suffice to say Mel was happy with it and the preparation of the evening had taken my mind off the murders in general. I'm not saying completely, because I'm sure you can tell, the day's events had caught up on me somewhat.

TWENTY SEVEN

Vanessa Brotherton was her name, and a mother of three, was what I gleaned from the news as I had been preparing the meal, but after that I'd tuned out; not intentionally, it just happened.

Once that was in my mind, with no doubt the sleep helping as well, I unconsciously started the mending process for my mind. I know what you mean, I'd killed Vanessa ages ago, but like I said the news had taken me aback, and I'm not a nasty person, so it affected me.

Not a nasty person you question? Well I'm not, I've got a family, I have friends and I'm kind to those around me; True I've done some terrible things, but are merely your actions what determine you to be a nasty person? If so there are plenty of people who would argue alongside me, about me being a lovely person.

Anyway, the news affected me and I needed time to recover, like always Mel was the best answer to this. By the time the evening was over, and we were cuddling in bed, a considerable amount of reparation had taken place.

Perhaps it is just farce, but I think a song comes to mind 'Love, Love changes everything.' Ah Michael Ball crooning fills my head. In my case there is some truth to those words, as without Mel I would have probably been arrested or put in hospital much sooner than I was.

As it is, I somehow managed to get on with my life, with very little interruption from Vanessa, Emma or that guy from Rough Wood.

Not everything went smoothly, and if I'm honest there were times when I could see from Mel's face that she thought something was wrong; on the odd occasion she asked me if everything was alright and I'm sure she had considered I was having an affair. Which is something I would never have done to Mel.

I think this world is amazing sometimes, I mean, I was involved, even if they didn't know it in a complete stranger's life. I was ultimately influential in the overall happiness of so many of the family left behind. Let's face it, I had caused untold torment for Vanessa's family whilst they ached and argued, dreamt and fashioned outcomes of what had happened to their mother/wife/daughter. Then in what must have been a massive release of some sort of emotion, they knew the truth that she was dead.

I sometimes wondered what that was like.

I still find it incredible that there are millions of people all engaged in their own little world, their own little lives, and they are completely unaware of how another person, a simple stranger....someone they have never known, someone they wouldn't recognise in the street can have such a dramatic affect on their little world and life; and they don't even consider this person, of the many worries they have, this person does not even come close to entering their thoughts.

I was that stranger.

I was the person they should've been worrying about, when they had been worrying whether the car would pass its MOT, or whether they had left the iron on when they left for work, they should have been worrying that I had a plan afoot, a plan that meant murder.

Still, I suppose life is like that, we never worry about the things that matter until it's too late, and we never say the things that are important until we never get a chance again.

Now, I'm sure you can imagine what has happened. This heightened attention to the murder, and moreover the murders that I have committed started that splinter of a niggle in my mind, I wasn't sure if it was the answer, but I needed to start to plan again, I knew it as I knew I needed breakfast.

TWENTY EIGHT

I think an important part of what happens now doesn't directly involve me, the two important people here are Chris and Clara.

As you know, Chris and Clara have been seeing each other some time now, and the weekend you've just heard about was starting to become a rarity, as Chris was found to be in Scotland on most weekends.

As you can imagine the relationship develops over a long period of time, and during this time I am slowly developing a plan, as I have described before; whilst drinking a cup of tea, or sitting on the toilet and sometimes while watching a film with Mel.

Everything is in my mind, I can't write anything down and sometimes the thought and plans have changed or been forgotten, sometimes I am unable to hold onto a thought to carry it to its conclusion, this process takes time. It does however take up my concentration and alleviate my guilt for a time.

Anyway, back to Chris and Clara.

So Chris is spending a lot of time up in Scotland and to be fair Clara comes down south fairly regularly too, and this has been going on for best part of a year now, to be honest it could be longer than that.

It didn't take me that long to plan what I was going to do, but as with anything it is the timing and location that is important, and there was about to be a big development as far as location is concerned.

I don't know that yet, but any plan I had made could quite easily be adapted to suit any situation, which is exactly what happened.

So Chris comes back from Scotland one weekend and we are all in the pub, it s Sunday and most of the gang appear at the pub at different times, we do all have families and need to see them too.

We are on our second pint of Abbot Ale when the rest of my group of friends have joined us, when Chris makes the announcement that he has decided that he is going to move to Glasgow. Chris goes on to say that not only is he going to move to Glasgow, but he has recently had job interviews and has got himself a new job in the city.

Although none of us were particularly shocked, as we had muted to each other that either Chris was going to move or Clara was, it must have struck as all as kind of strange that we were going to lose one of us up north.

To be honest, it meant a lot to me to see Chris happy, and although it seemed I would be losing one of my best friends, I also felt happy that he had found someone to be happy with and could build his own life.

As he had already claimed himself a Scottish job, he literally had a month and a half to prepare everything else, including handing in his notice for his Midlands job.

It was a lot of preparation and although the majority was left to Chris and Clara, we all chipped in with different things to make the move easier. Before we knew the time was upon us and Chris was driving around in a long wheel base Ford Transit, which he had hired to take his belongings up north.

Again, it was a Sunday, me Chris and Mouse turned up at Chris' parents house in order to drag a load of furniture into the back of the transit and make the move up to Glasgow. All in all there wasn't that much and within a couple of hours we were on the motorway, the three of us cramped into the front of the Transit.

A couple of packets of Haribo sour sweets, a packet of Minstrels and a couple of cans of Coke between us, we were soon hankering for something substantial to eat. We were about 150 miles into the 280 mile journey and we decided to pull off the motorway at Tebay, Westmorland Services, in the Lake District.

Unlike any other services I have been to, Tebay offers good food at reasonable prices and was a delight to stay at. If I was going to be making future trips to Glasgow, I would have to remember to save coming off the motorway until getting to Tebay.

Before long we were back on the motorway and continuing the arduous journey, it's amazing how quickly 5 hours goes by when you're having a laugh and a joke, and we were soon driving along the M74 heading more precisely to the Dennistoun area just outside Glasgow City.

The flat is on the second floor of a tenement building. Lugging a sofa that Chris had acquired from a family member, up the four flights of stairs was no mean feat; me and Mouse were out of breath by the time we got the sofa to the front door of the flat.

Clara was already at the flat and had prepared a pot of tea for us when we arrived. I took my cup and gulped the liquid down, Chris and Mouse struggled getting the sofa through the door and I surveyed the flat.

Seeing as it didn't look too big from the outside, inside it was like the Tardis. With high ceilings and large rooms, the flat was much more than I had imagined it would be. Perhaps not in the nicest part of Glasgow, but all in all it was a pleasant flat and already had a homely feel with just a kettle, a few cups and tea bags.

As I was standing in what was to become the living room, looking down onto the street from the my second floor vantage point, I was struck by a notion, it was a notion that made me excited and at the same time made me nervous. It needed more thought, but it was a firm premise of a notion.

Remember another important point. I'm a murderer at large, concealed within this innocent and polite exterior. Bubbling just beneath the surface was my murderous intent, and as you can tell by now, premeditation is high up on my list, but I'm not going to let it take up much of my thought right now; we still had to get the fridge into the flat.

The laborious ins and outs of what happened next in Glasgow is quite inconsequential at the moment, and to be honest it's not something I'll come back to. Suffice to say that Chris and Clara settle in to their new home and there is always a place for me if I want to visit.

I do visit Scotland again, in fact I go quite regularly, which is something I will obviously have to come back to, because as you can imagine, it's a whole new city, where it would appear on initial investigation I have absolutely no ties.

Perfect.

TWENTY NINE

Like I said, I will be coming back to Glasgow, and yes, murder is afoot, but that isn't something for right now.

It was weird to start with, sure we were all in the pub as usual, but there was one of us missing, and it felt a little different.

Now something happened that I had never would have thought of, but it goes to show what a small place this world is.

As you know, in order to keep the bills paid I sell my life by the hour to an insurance company, and at the moment my life wasn't being sold for enough money, and I was looking for promotion. I had spent long enough at the company and although the pay grade had increased each year, I wanted to make a bigger jump in salary, if not only to pay for some of the things which I expected, or perhaps would unexpectedly crop up during the next murder.

There was a job opening coming up according to an internet email, and it sounded right up my street, as it was a managerial position in an area I'd spent the most of my time in the company. It takes a certain kind of person to stay calm and polite to obnoxious people.

I emailed the appropriate people, and before long I had an interview date due by the end of the week. Apparently, according to the rumours, the person leaving would be in on the interview, and to be fair I knew her already anyway, so wasn't bothered by it. I heard of the other people who had applied, and to be honest I gave myself a good chance, and for an extra five grand a year, I was quite excited about the prospect.

Mel was excited for me too, and she was already geeing me up about being right for the job and saying that by the same time the following week we'd be having a celebration. She was incredibly supportive through everything; I knew, one day, I would marry her.

I was also planning that come the new job or not, I'd arrange something nice and would pop the question to Mel, then cross my fingers.

It was only on the Tuesday, with the interview looming on Friday, I was at my desk and had just finished quite a complex calculation in order to obtain a surrender value figure for a client's with profits insurance policy. These were never good reading, especially when you work out how much had been paid in, the best thing in all cases was stay the entire term, but I suppose in all cases it wasn't possible. I was about to start filling in the blanks of my prewritten document outlining the figures when my manager came and stood behind me. She placed her hand on my shoulder and asked if she could have a quick word.

The office was fairly open plan, there were sectioned off areas of the office which were obtained by non permanent walls that could be moved at will and were only about 5'10" high, so you could see over them if necessary.

My manager had her own separate room from the main office, I had locked my computer terminal, as spoof emails from colleagues were very popular and sometimes incredibly embarrassing…I mean, obviously, that data protection was at my forethought.

I walked into her office and closed the door, she was sat behind her desk and offered me the chair positioned the opposite her, the other side of her desk. The chair I sat in was marginally lower than her own leather adjustable one, to put me in my place I'd imagine.

Heather started to speak, her voice was lower and softer than usual, she was obviously about to say something I needed to keep to myself, something she didn't want anyone else to know.

With the closed door session over, I left Heather's office. It was difficult to not feel conspicuous, especially with such an open plan office, in reality everyone was pretty much engrossed in their own work. When I got back to my desk Jane gave me a sort of a backward nod, she lifted he head and raised her eyebrows in a question of what that had all been about. She was on the phone when I returned, hence the body language question.

I sat down at my desk and unlocked my computer, I was going to have to make something up when Jane finally got round to asking me what I had talked about with Heather, which meant I would have to lie, and you know how difficult I find lying.

THIRTY

I was thinking about what had been said in the meeting during the drive home, it was only going to take me about twenty five minutes to get home, and when I did I knew that Mel would be there already. Mel was a teacher assistant at a school in Bilston, so she had far less distance to travel to get to my house, and with it being a Tuesday she generally came straight to mine.

When I pulled up outside my house I saw that Mel's car was parked in the opposite bay, my heart gave a little flutter knowing she was already at home.

The door opened before I could get my key in the door, and Mel was giving me a large grin, I took a step inside and gave her a hug and a kiss. She turned and headed for the kitchen, I watched her bum as she walked away.

I closed the door and followed her into the kitchen, by the time I got there Mel already had the kettle starting to boil, as if reading my mind.

I took hold of Mel around her waist whilst she was stood at the kitchen unit with her back to me, and pulled her against me, I gave her a kiss on her exposed neck. Whilst in this embrace I started to tell Mel all about what had happened at work.

I was making a cup of tea for us both as I was telling her the rest of what had been said, two sugars for Mel. She had a fantastic figure and was a size 10, yet she had two sugars in her tea, one of those lucky people who can eat anything without impact. I took toll of how she looked as I stirred the tea, she was beautiful to me.

Dinner was already cooking in the oven, and we sat in the living room talking until it was ready. We sat and ate dinner at a small table that we used as our dining table. It was big enough for the two of us, it was big enough for four if it was extended, but as it was the two of us fitted just snugly.

101

I enjoyed being close to Mel, not only did she have a wonderful figure, but she was pretty. I often found myself looking at her just thinking 'wow'. I truly felt lucky to be with her.

Mel was as excited as I was about the news I'd had from work, but this wasn't the time to talk about work. I try to keep those two things separate, with the exception of the good news I had.

On a Tuesday Mel usually stayed over at mine, so as you can imagine, we spent the evening together, mostly wrapped up in each others arms on the sofa watching a film that was on Freeview. Not that it is important but I think it was Fight Club.

The alarm clock woke me at 7am, and I turned over and hit the snooze button, I wasn't fully awake or fully aware of my actions or thoughts, my autonomic reaction was to turn over and take hold of Mel.

By the time the snooze had gone off for a second time, both Mel and I were awake. We were holding each other, Mel was on her side, and I was on my back, her head was resting on my chest, my right arm was encircling her, holding us together.

It was an incredible feeling to be so interwoven with another person, to feel that desire for closeness and intimacy. I'm not talking about sex, I'm talking about that sharing of each other, that feeling when your bodies touch and you appear to be on exactly the same wavelength, that you could read each other's minds, a joining between two people, to become one.

THIRTY ONE

Innocent smoothies are lovely, instead of orange juice I took Mel a glass of Pomegranate smoothie, apparently made from juice and never ever from concentrate. Mel told me that this was good for you, and could be counted as one of your five a day portions of fruit/vegetables you should have.

The bacon was cooking downstairs and I opened the bedroom door, the noise made Mel turn over and fidget, but she had obviously dropped off to sleep again while I had been downstairs. Her eyes were closed and she had a kind of sublime grin on her face.

I crept across the bedroom and placed the glass of smoothie on the bedside cabinet, Mel didn't budge, I retraced my steps out of the bedroom and gently closed the door.

A thought encroached on my serene mind as I took hold of the spatula to tackle the bacon cooking in the pan. It was the handle, a handle that fitted snugly in my hand, a handle that extended out well beyond my hand, similar to hammer. Emma Jackson.

I can't tell you exactly why it happened but it did, but holding that spatula gave me an eerie and horrid recollection of that torrid time in that quiet lane in Essington. Sometimes I hate how the brain works.

It was the weekend at last and this meant we could have a little lie in, a lie in was a contradiction in terms. Our bodies were so conditioned into waking at a specific time that usually they awoke without the alarm at the normal time anyway. Believe me though, if this was a week day I would be asleep until midday some as my body could get me in trouble, a weird but true occurrence.

Anyway, back to the bacon.

I finished off cooking the bacon and prepared the sandwich to Mel's liking, a little splash of HP brown sauce. This time when I opened the bedroom door, Mel had stirred awake and was sipping from the smoothie, she sat up in bed as I approached with the plate of bacon sandwich.

For the rest of the day we had nothing planned for a change, we usually had to fit things in our weekends off but this weekend there was nothing, it was a lovely relaxed Saturday, we had nowhere to go and all day to get there.

Well, I say we had a relaxed day, Mel did, and I portrayed having one, but the spatula incident had stayed with me, and I had moments of slipping back into thinking of Emma Jackson. I obviously didn't say anything to Mel, but the lapses had bought about a migraine. I blamed a glass of full fat milk I had drunk earlier in the day, but I knew that wasn't true, there was only one reason. Emma Jackson.

With the migraine in full swing I headed off to bed early and tried to get to sleep. The pain was the sort of pain that you can't ignore, especially in bed, it bought with it a nauseous feeling.

I don't remember dropping off to sleep, I remember tossing and turning trying to get comfortable, while holding my head, or clasping my bicep over my eyes and letting my forearm collapse around my ear. However it was my alarm that woke me the following morning.

Mel had managed to clamber into bed and fall asleep next to me and I hadn't noticed or murmured in my slumber.

The morning bought with it a fresh feeling for my head, and the alarm, which I had accidentally left on from my working week had awoken me to a world without pain. It was a relief. It's funny, while you're healthy you don't really appreciate it and quite often take it for granted, when you are ill, you long for that return to normal.

While lying on my back, Mel taking deep breaths next to me I made a decision, a decision that would lead to another death, another life to be lost.

THIRTY TWO

During the following week, I kept my head down at work and avoided much of the speculation about what was going on, and I gave Chris a call, luckily he was free this coming weekend, and I decided I'd take a trip up north, I had something to plan.

It had been raining, it had been raining hard. I looked out of the second floor window and the street below seemed to reflect back at me, it was so wet. I could see my car from above, I was sure the T-bar roof of the MR2 would be leaking, the rain had been terrible overnight.

Chris and Clara had both gone to work, leaving me with a key for the flat so I could come and go as I please.

I had decided to take the Friday as annual leave, so I had travelled after work on the Thursday so I could complete the six hour journey up to Glasgow while the motorways were clear. This meant I had an entire day to myself. I wanted to learn my way around the city and get accustomed to the accent.

I took a stroll from the tenement flat and towards the city centre. Dennistoun is about a half an hour walk from the main city centre, luckily I'd packed my waterproof jacket; it was wet.

I suppose I could have quite easily have caught one of the black cabs for the city and had a dry, five minute ride into the city, but it was only a single road along Duke Street, and it led directly to the city, and I wanted to see what was around me.

Isn't strange how some places have an importance, and that you don't automatically realise the first time you are there.

Like I said, I was walking along Duke Street, and I reached a point where the old slaughterhouse used to be, this is now a large open space of concrete and rubble, just waiting to be developed. Opposite this vast expanse I saw a hotel. It had an ornate red brick outer to the building and it looked very grand, and I could imagine that at some point in its past it had been the home to a wealthy businessman.

The Duke Hotel, was covered in ornate carvings into the red brick, it had large windows, and a design that said 'I was built to last'. It was a pleasing building to look at from outside.

I crossed over the road, with an intent to go inside and check the place out.

The door I approached, naturally was locked, as I often find whenever I approach a doorway with a multiple of doors that could be opened, I pick the wrong one.

I pushed and pulled on the handle of the first door a couple of times before this realisation set in though. I approached the second door and a momentary indecision of whether to push or pull came over me, when I grabbed the handle and gave it a push. The door opened.

I walked inside to quite a grand lobby, half way up the wall was a kind of mosaic made up of small tiles, and on the floor, again tiles covered it, to a large oak reception desk.

There was a woman behind the reception desk, probably mid forties, not unattractive but had obviously seen her best days some years ago.

As I approached she welcomed me with a toothy smile, "Welcome to The Duke Hotel, is there anything we can do for you just now?" she asked, her accent was thick Scottish, a type of Glaswegian that was hard on the ears and difficult to catch the exact words.

I told her I was just looking for a place to stay in the future, and she offered me a business card and small brochure, which must have been designed and printed in the late eighties.

The number had been crossed out and re-written, to show the

now up to date telephone number of the hotel, I said I'd keep hold of it and would give them a call when I needed a room. I left pleased that I had found the location, so that was at least a part of my mind that could rest.

As I strode along the remainder of Duke Street and into George Street my mind was racing with the possibilities of what could be done at that old hotel.

Before I knew it I found myself in George Square, and didn't really know where things were in the city, luckily there were a couple of sign posts which pointed me in the right direction. I took a mental note of where I was and what was around me, so that I knew I could find my way back.

I had a wander around the city taking in some of the sights and a mental picture of where things were, and after a couple of hours, I headed back to the flat.

One things was for sure though, in the time I had taken around the city, with my mind racing on probable plans and possibilities, I had come to a decision, a decision that would lead to a death, a murder and the ultimate relaxation for that niggle in my mind.

The rest of my stay with Chris involved a lot of beer, a few games on his Playstation, and a lot of talking about the kind of inconsequential rubbish that only a couple of drunken guys together can talk about. Chris had been my friend for so many years now, even though we didn't see each other as often as we used to there was a connection that would always remain. We always got on well together.

THIRTY THREE

Location, location, location. Such an important factor in so many things and it's the same with murder, especially if you want to keep the police from the door, and as you know, this is one of the main things that occupies my mind when considering a murder.

The drive back to the Midlands, was, to be honest, a bit of a bind. Traffic around Manchester was appalling, and as ever there were plenty of roadworks, bringing my steady 70mph journey down to 40mph quite regularly. Annoying.

With the roadworks and sheer volume of traffic around Manchester, it took me nearly six and a half hours to get home. When I got back inside, I closed the door, dropped my rucksack on the floor and headed straight towards bed, the journey had given me a bit of headache. As I started tucking myself into bed, I sent Mel a text message from my mobile phone, saying I was home safely and feeling knackered, and decided to get my eyes tested the following weekend.

Now, the time between now and the murder is mostly inconsequential, so I'm not going to bother telling you about it, it was just me living my life, planning a murder.

It didn't take long for the preparation to be done, however there was a snag, Chris and Clara were away many weekends, so picking a weekend when they were available and that suited me and Mel, was difficult.

Saying what I have, all of my thoughts and preparation and the general living of my life, took that little niggle away from me. Being preoccupied with planning, and living, stopped those thoughts that made me get caught up in what I had done already.

So each time something like the spatula incident occurs, or I get caught up in my thoughts about what I have done, there is only one answer, and that is to plan to murder someone else, it becomes a necessity in order to keep myself sane, and to live my life like others do.

Anyway, it was probably a good four months before the weekends married up so that I could take another trip up to Glasgow, I decided there was a few things I needed to do before I left as the time grew nearer.

The only internet café I could think of was in Wolverhampton, so the weekend before I planned to go up north I spent an hour or so in the internet café.

Now I'm not gifted when it comes to computers and the internet, but I know enough to know that if I searched and ordered the kind of thing I was looking for at home, using my own details, someone, somewhere would pick up on it and I'd be behind bars before I knew it.

No, I'm no genius but I'm not an idiot.

Besides, there was no way I was going to provide my personal details, not the real ones, not for this kind of purchase. I wanted the hotel to think I was someone completely different, and one of the only ways to be sure that no-one had any of my real details was to order things online from an internet café, and to pay for everything in cash.

Luckily I had opened that savings account, and true to my own word had kept the funds flowing into it since my last murder, and to be fair I had quite a decent amount saved, easily enough for what was needed.

Getting hold of the money was easy, the bank had provided a cashpoint card to be used in a hole in the wall. It was just a matter of withdrawing the money, which I did before leaving up north. Everything was set in motion.

THIRTY FOUR

The wind whistled through a small gap in the window, the noise almost sounded like someone blowing a muffled whistle. The flat was quiet and light poured into the room from the large floor to ceiling window that the flat boasted.

I felt quite comfortable walking around the flat naked. No-one was home apart from me, and being on the first floor no-one could look down upon my nakedness.

I took a shower and left the flat fairly early, it was only half past nine and I was at the front door of the Duke hotel. I still managed to give the doors a familiar push and pull to find the right one, and entered into the lobby.

I had withdrawn the money for the room from the cashpoint and when I arrived at the main desk I was greeted with a warm smile from the male standing behind the counter.

I explained that I had made a reservation and gave my false name, to be honest I can't remember what it was so let's just say I claimed to be Dave Johnson. Despite the ostentatious exterior of the hotel and the lovely mosaic interior the hotel was quite a colloquial place, family run. Anyway, I booked in and paid for the room, they said I could pay after my stay, but I wanted to get the payment out of the way, obviously I paid in cash. The hotelier passed me a key that was attached to a large brass key fob, upon which was the room number, 13.

I looked at the fob and chuckled to myself, 'unlucky for some, number 13' it certainly was going to be unlucky for someone, little did I know then that I would be included in that unfortunate superstition about the number 13.

I took my bag, and headed for the stairs I had been given quick directions from the man behind the counter, and headed the way he said. It was a short flight of stairs up and I followed a corridor to my left, half way down there was the room. Number

13.

The door opened into a fairly spacious room, it was en suite, which I specifically requested. The carpet was a tough looking fabric in a neutral beige colour and the walls were magnolia. There were a couple paintings up on the wall to give the room a homely feel, but to be honest it was a little sparse.

I closed the door behind me and dropped my bag on the floor, I took a wander around to examine the place and see what kind of shower gel and shampoo was in the bathroom. The white towels neatly stacked at the end of the bed a custom of hotel rooms.

The bathroom was a good size which was important, as you'll see in a while, with a basin, and combined bath and shower. Above the basin was a mirror, with one of those small lights above it with a cord to turn the light on and off hanging at the side.

I went over to the bed and checked out how much spring was in the mattress, not that I was going to be using it.

I put the TV on and went on sat on the bed, then I thought about the towels that my feet were resting on, and with a leap in my heart as I had almost forgotten, I went and put most of them in the bathroom, leaving one of them at the foot of the bed. I had almost forgotten an important part of my plan.

I was in the hotel room for about an hour, when there was a knock on the door, when I opened the door there was a woman standing there, quite pretty, who introduced herself as Mandie. I stood aside and she walked past me into the hotel room, I closed the door.

THIRTY FIVE

I turned from the door but when I went to speak with Mandie I
realised that my mouth was dry in anticipation of what was
happening, and that I didn't really know what to say, I had
planned, but I hadn't planned the small details like this.

Funnily Mandie must have been used to this kind of situation
and made the small talk for me, she found it quite funny and
thought my dry mouth was down to shyness as opposed to
anything else. Which in turn was quite funny.

Mandie had a bag with her, and started to get out a couple of
dresses, she placed these on the bed, I noticed that both were
PVC, both were black and both had holes, for prominent points
of the female anatomy.

I didn't really know where to look to be honest, and I felt
incredibly embarrassed, the escort agency had been very polite
and everything had been arranged with the utmost of
confidentiality and discreteness, but here and now, watching this
woman get ready for some kind of sexual encounter, I felt self
conscious and embarrassed.

Mandie told me that I was naughty for watching her and that she
was going to go to the bathroom to get changed, I reminded her
that the bathroom lock was broken and didn't work; it did of
course work, but I didn't want that bathroom door to be locked.

Mandie went into the bathroom after I had pointed to one of the
black dresses and closed the door, reassuring I heard that she
didn't even try to lock the door, obviously she felt relaxed in my
company already; the £250.00 had already been taken from off
the bedside cabinet without a single word, no doubt helped
towards the reassurance that this was going to be easy money.

I didn't wait long, my heart was in my mouth and my hands
were shaking as I approached the bathroom door, my adrenaline
already forcing that fight or flight emotion out of me before

anything had begun.

The towel that I had left on the end of the bed was in my hands, I turned the handle and walked into the bathroom.

Mandie was leaning over the basin, looking in the mirror, she was naked, completely naked with her 'normal' clothes on the floor and the dress I had chosen draped over the bath. She looked at me as I walked in and made some kind of comment about continuing to be naughty, but to be honest my mind was on other things. I was surprised that she took me seeing her naked without the blink of an eye.

As I was walking I was saying something about the towel in my hands, and that its place was in the bathroom with the others, she looked at where I had placed the other towels earlier, then looked back at the mirror turning her back to me as I continued towards them.

With her back to me, I saw the opportunity I was after, I quickly and surprisingly deftly, took the towel between both of my hands, it was a fraction of a second before the towel was around her neck, I gave it a sharp pull to pull her off balance, her immediate reaction was to grab at the towel around her throat.

Now that she was off balance I was able to smash her head hard against the mirror, this broke and although I couldn't see it from my angle I knew she was bleeding I could see it dripping into the basin. The blow to her head must have numbed her brain and her thoughts, as she was moaning incoherently. It should have done something to her thoughts, I used all of my strength to smash her head into the mirror.

She was breathing heavily and I was breathing heavily too, one person struggling against another is extremely hard work, you may not have any idea what I'm talking about, and hopefully you never do, especially this kind exhaustive behaviour.

Mandie was only slight but keeping control of her was a real struggle, I was pulling hard on the towel, and I knew the airway

114

was closed as I could feel her trying to draw air in, but could hear that nothing was getting through.

Her body was autonomically thrashing in panic of not being able to get any air. All of the thrashing and struggling sent us to the floor and I was on top her, pulling hard on the towel, her fingers were scratching lines of blood through her skin of her neck as she tried to get some kind of purchase on the towel, but it was tight, as tight as both of my arms pulling on it could muster.

My arms were aching and I gave a brief respite of pulling and in a dramatic change, I slammed her head against the bathroom floor, it wasn't really her head though, it was her face that made most of the contact with the floor. I heard a crack, as her nose broke, and within a few seconds the struggling stopped, I could see that some of the edges of the towel were now stained red, and I wasn't sure if it was from cuts made from the mirror or the breaking of her nose. Obviously something about her broken nose aided the death, whether it somehow stopped an air coming in to her lungs at all, or whether the break had sent cartilage and bone up into her brain I don't know, but it was complete.

I clambered off her body and sat on the bathroom floor, looking at what I had done, she was almost lying diagonally across the floor, and if someone had asked me to walk into the bathroom earlier and draw a chalk outline of a murder victim, the way she looked now would have been exactly as I would have drawn, I could use her body as a death pose template.

Her one arm was under her body presumably still trying to take hold of the towel, her other arm was outstretched above her head, and her legs were almost identical, with one bent at the knee and the other outstretched straight.

As I started to come to my senses and for the 'normal' thinking part of my brain to come back to the forefront, I realised that in the melee, I had cuts to my hand, either from the glass of the mirror or from the bang against the floor, also that I was thirsty and starving.

115

As I went to stand up, my legs were wobbling, and I had to hold onto the basin to steady myself, there was blood in the basin, either mine or hers, which smudged as my fingers took hold of the basin.

On unsteady legs through both exhaustion and nervousness, I walked out of the bathroom and closed the door behind me, I didn't want her looking at me, or me her.

I almost collapsed onto the bed, and picked up the telephone and pressed the button in the middle, a male voice answered with two words "Room service". I ordered steak and chips with a pot of tea, and they said it would be about twenty minutes. I replaced the receiver and lay back onto the pillow, my eyes were starting to close.

There was a knock on the door.

It could have only been two or three minutes at the most, so it couldn't be the steak, a horrible thought rushed through my mind that the commotion from the room had alerted someone and that it was now police at the door, asking if everything was ok, I was almost immediately in a state of panic, this was it, this was the start of a long prison sentence.

Another noise, it wasn't the door at all, but was coming from the bathroom, I opened the door and to my amazement her dead body had turned over and her horrifically bloody face was staring up at the ceiling, her mouth was gaping open and I could see that she was drawing in breaths. I suddenly realised that the dead body was alive.

I rushed over and did the only thing I could think of, I mean this was not an eventuality I had planned for, and it wasn't something I was expecting to have to do. Now this seems incredibly harsh, but you have to remember the situation I am in.

There is a partially murdered, completely naked woman in the bathroom of a hotel room that I am the only other occupant of, there is someone downstairs cooking a steak to my medium rare

116

liking who would be coming into this cosy little picture within minutes, and yes, a long prison sentence would loom.

I stamped, I stamped hard, two three or four times, I don't know, on her exposed throat, whatever, if anything was working within that soft and delicate passageway for air and food was now a completely crumpled broken mess of tissue and bone, all attempts to continue breathing again stopped. Her eyes were open, staring blankly at the ceiling light.

I didn't need to check her pulse, I waved my hand in front of her eyes, and there was no reaction at all, she was dead at last.

I left the bathroom again and closed the door, excitement of this nature has a profound affect on the body and mind and my tiredness was now completely gone, my hunger and thirst remained.

I again collapsed back onto the bed in the room, my head nestled onto the pillow and despite me thinking my tiredness had gone, my eyes started to close. It may have only been a blink, or it may have been a power nap, I don't know but what seemed like as soon as my eyes were closed, there was a knock at the door.

I wasn't completely sure that the knock had come from the door and my mind slipped to the horrific image of the body in the bathroom, and I dearly hoped that I wouldn't have to return to that room. There was again a knock at the door, and a voice from the other side proclaimed that it was room service.

I went to the door and opened it to find the man from reception with a trolley containing the steak and chips, the smell immediately gave my saliva glands a twinge and I felt my mouth watering. I took the trolley and the male at the door asked if I had received a guest, he gave me a kind of knowing grin. My heart went straight into my mouth, I think I managed to say that she was in the bathroom, but it must have been a very stilted response.

With the door closed again I felt a little less nervous, I no longer fancied the chips but I gulped the steak down very quickly and what remained I left on the plate and left the plate on the bed.

It may be hard to believe that I could act like this, a little strange, knowing what you do about me already, but I agree that it isn't the behaviour of a 'normal' person, I mean what kind of person does it take to be able to eat steak immediately after killing someone?

Thinking back I should have had the steak well done.

THIRTY SIX

I don't want to ruin things for you, but I must say, things go quite pear shaped for me with this murder, I'm not going to tell you the exact extent just yet, but suffice to say that I certainly feel the heat of my actions. I'll come back to the details later, not too long, but not just yet.

I had a healthy pace back to Chris' flat, I didn't want to get caught out in the street, and I didn't know how long it would take for the staff at the hotel to find the body. Granted I had left the 'don't disturb' sign on the handle of the door outside, and I had made my way out of the hotel with no-one at reception to see me go.

When I closed the door the Chris' flat I almost slumped against it, as though my body weight could keep everything I had done at bay. I did the first thing I could think of when I got on, I gave a Mel a call, I needed to hear a friendly voice.

The call went straight to answer phone, Mel was at work and I should have expected her phone to be off, it was strange but I felt such a close association with Mel that I believed just the sound of her voice could cure my ills.

My ills were far deeper and far more tragic that even Mel's voice could cure, I went to the flat's cramped kitchen and made a cup of tea, I don't know why I made it, because I knew really that it would remain un-drunk.

I sat on one of the brown sofa in the living room, the tea remained on the floor and the tv blared away, Tim Robinson was explaining about some kind of trench that the time team had dug to see if an ancient village had existed on a plot of field some time ago in existence.

Clara was the first to get home and I think I held up the persona that everything was normal quite easily, this was absolutely destroyed when Chris returned. Within a minute or two, he was asking what was wrong, as it appeared that I was different.

Isn't funny how those who know us best can pick up on any kind of difference in our attitude and feelings, its as if those who are close to us can actually empathise and feel the kind of emotion we are feeling ourselves. Chris couldn't feel this emotion though, he had never killed someone, he had certainly never killed someone in the horrific manner I had done just minutes before.

Chris was astute enough though and in tune with my behavioural patterns that he had gleaned over the past twelve years to know that something wasn't quite right with me. He knew that it wasn't anything extraordinary, but something was wrong.

The fact that he didn't think it was anything extraordinary was testament to my own inner discipline, because I was shitting myself, I was struggling to keep my emotions in check and unless I was careful, my behaviour and deeds of the day may slip out.

Chris offered me a drink of beer and turned on his Playstation, we played a game that we had started probably a year earlier, and before long not only had his belief that something was wrong had disappeared, but my own feelings of wrong doing had dissipated.

Within a couple of hours I was tucking myself into the sleeping bag I had bought with me, which nestled nicely on the sofa in the spare room of the flat. I had spoken to Mel after she had finished work, and as I tucked myself in, I sent her a text describing how much she meant to me and how much I loved her.

It must be incomprehensible to you to hear how I conduct myself following a murder, I'm sure you think that you would be different, I'm sure that you think that you would perhaps break down in an uncontrollable heap, or perhaps that you would behave in a different way, that you would take your own life, or even that you would own up to it. Well I'll tell you something, and that is that the human response to keep oneself safe and secure overrides all things it puts everything else behind it. Sleep came quite quickly, and as usual, I couldn't tell you if a dreamt or not, I don't put much faith into reading things into dreams anyway, so it wouldn't matter if I could remember them or not.

I awoke to the sound of Chris clattering around the kitchen, I knew it was Chris as I could hear the odd profanity here and there when he knocked something over or stubbed his toe, I also heard the welcoming sound of the kettle boiling and hoped a nice hot cup of tea would be forthcoming fairly soon. I made my way into the bathroom just so that Chris knew I was awake and tat he wouldn't be disturbing me by brining in the tea.

I returned to the bedroom and as I walked through the hallway Chris shouted out a 'morning' to acknowledge me being upright.

I tucked myself back into my sleeping bag, and a minute or so later there was a knock on the door and Chris came in holding a steaming cup of tea. He returned to his own bedroom and I could hear him talking to Clara.

I drank the tea quickly, and enjoyed the warm feeling as the tea passed down my throat, as soon as it was gone I immediately fancied another cup.

Now you have to remember that yesterday I had committed a murder, obviously there were many things going around my head, but I also had to make sure that I behaved normally towards everyone else, otherwise a horrible discovery about me may be made.

I wondered what was going on at the hotel as I walked towards the kitchen to make another cup of tea for myself. I mean, someone must have discovered the body by now, the maid or manager or whoever, must have made the grim discovery in Room 13.

As I filled the kettle I started to think about a Columbo styled detective overlooking the crime scene, smoking his cigar and making a mental note of al the most important factors of the room. I plugged the kettle in and switched it on. I heard Chris shout that there was another cup in the pot. I flicked the switch on the kettle back off and tipped the stainless steel tea pot over the cup and was glad to see the last of the tea fill the cup up to the top. Result.

I wondered when I would get to hear anything about this murder, I wondered if anything would be on the news yet, as I would imagine something like this would make the news.

I took my second cup of tea back to the bedroom and sipped this one slowly, despite wanting to know what was happening, I didn't want to get up properly yet, and avoided putting the television on.

I dozed for another hour or so.

THIRTY SEVEN

Now I didn't really hear anything about what I had done on the Saturday, after the morning we spent the day out of the house and I didn't see the television or a newspaper for the rest of the day, and as I was there for the weekend, it was the Sunday that put the frights up me.

We all seemed to rise at the same sort of time, whether that is some kind of pack instinct from when we were herding animals I don't know, but it was about 09.30am that we all started to get up.

We met in the living room and Chris came to meet Clara and I with a hot cup of tea, the kind of ritual that should begin any morning. We were in our nightwear, Chris fashioning a ruby coloured bathrobe, and me in my shorts and a t-shirt.

I had not long finished my tea, and a news bulletin came on the television, not a breaking news story type, just one of the regular on the hour news updates. However, this update did mention a police scene at Duke Street, Glasgow following some kind of incident, the details of which the police weren't releasing to the press.

Clara was intrigued about what she had seen on the news and encouraged me and Chris to get our clothes on so we could have a walk down to Duke Street and rubber neck at what was going on.

I was obviously reluctant, I naturally gave other reasons, as opposed to the fact that I was the culprit of this particular incident, to avoid going to the scene.

Clara was insistent that she wanted to go and have a look, so within 20 minutes we were out in the street walking towards The Duke Hotel. I couldn't help but think about Mandie, the police would probably be taking photographs about now, and I had left her in a terrible state.

I actually had no idea of the stage of the police investigation, gleaning all I know about what happens at a crime scene from CSI and films, no doubt the reality was much different. In fact I hoped it would be different, because they usually find the murderer in an hour.

As we reached The Duke Hotel, it was clear that a media circus had already begun, and there were people standing around waiting to see what was going on. The police were behind a mass of blue and white tape, which sectioned off the front of the hotel, as well as the entire part of a section of footpath directly outside.

I really didn't want to be there, don't they say a murderer always returns to the scene of the crime, well that bullshit, because it had taken a great deal to drag me back to this awful place. It was only my fear that if a protested too much, that it may appear odd, that I hadn't stuck my heels in and refused to go.

So although I was back at the scene of the crime, this was and is the only time it happens, lets remember I want to avoid that room with the metal bars for as long as possible.

There were journalists at the line of the police cordon, testing the officers on the line with how close they could get without being told to stay further back, I'm sure The Duke Hotel had never seen as many cameras and interest, however I'm pretty sure it was not the kind of publicity The Duke Hotel would have wanted.

I made an excuse and left the hub of excitement outside the hotel and went to a local shop to get a packet of painkillers and a bottle of Lucozade, I wasn't feeling all that bright, which would be the ideal excuse to get back to the flat.

I returned to the crowd outside the hotel swigging my bottle of Lucozade, I stood next to Chris and Clara and told them my excuse about a nasty headache, I borrowed a key from Chris and took a slow wander back to the flat.

124

I was glad to be back in the sanctuary of the flat, it had felt awful to be back at the hotel. It wasn't long before Chris and Clara returned, and I was able to put what I had done and the returning to the crime to the back of my mind with some conversation about something else, I can't tell you what we talked about, because I don't remember; I just have that feeling that whatever it was, was a welcome change to the subject I had been concentrating on.

To be honest I was quite desperate to get back home and to Mel, and the weekend seemed to drag on, well that's how I remember it anyway, and when Sunday afternoon came I was soon in my car, and racing down the motorway to get back home.

I wasn't expecting the kind of 'welcome home' that I actually got.

THIRTY EIGHT

'Welcome Home' isn't that meant to be a warm greeting? Well I have to say that my return to the Midlands was not a 'Welcome Home' it was more like a bucket of cold water in the face; panic and shock.

Like an unwanted visitor before dinner, a telephone call asking if you want double glazing when your favourite TV program is on, my 'Welcome Home' was just as impressive.

Mel was out with her friends, in consolation to having to go back to work. It wasn't that which had turned things so bad, I trusted Mel implicitly, no the problem, the dread, was the news. Now bearing in mind that Glasgow is nearly 300 miles away, you wouldn't necessarily think that a murder committed there would be news in the Midlands but it was.

I walked into the house and switched the television on, there's something about an empty quiet house that makes it a more foreboding place, even though it is home.

You can guess what I did next no doubt, and that's to put the kettle on, there's nothing like settling in with a nice cup of tea. I was standing in the kitchen, stirring the tea bag, when I overheard the news, broadcasting out into the empty living room.

The news caught my attention, it caught my attention to such a degree, that open mouthed I walked from the kitchen into the living room, still clutching the teaspoon from stirring the tea. I stood looking at the television in horror.

All of a sudden the horrid truth of what I had done hit me, not only the truth of what I had done, but the truth that I was eventually going to be found out. Its weird, but the first thing that crossed my mind, was nothing to do with myself, but what would happen to my house and my car while I was in jail.

126

What I was looking at was me, I was on television, and not in a way that I had ever wanted to be, what I was watching was the CCTV from the hotel that had apparently captured a murderer as he left the hotel in Glasgow. I was absolutely shocked to see myself, moreover that the footage was already out in the public domain.

First of all I didn't know what to do with myself, I didn't know whether I should just hand myself in, whether I should go and find Mel and say my goodbye before the police caught me, see my family, see my friends.

I think it was particularly lucky that Mel was out, because no matter how I've dealt with the things I have done in the past there would have been no way I could have suppressed what I was feeling, which would have been the biggest giveaway that I was guilty.

I gathered my thoughts, I needed to think about what I was going to do, and I needed to think about the likelihood of being discovered.

I went back to the kitchen and put the milk in the tea.

I must have a remarkable constitution for putting things in order in my mind, I don't know whether we all have the ability, but its something that I have inside of me.

I sat on the sofa, cup in my hand, watching the TV and thinking, I don't know what was on the TV, as the news had finished, its effect lingering with me more than most who had seen the broadcast.

As usual the tea remained un-drunk, and when I came to my senses I wasn't quite sure how much time had elapsed, but I had a plan. It wasn't a sophisticated one, it was the same plan that I always used.

I'd say nothing.
If someone mentioned the murder I'd feign that I hadn't seen the

news. I wondered if anyone around here, or Chris would put two and two together and recognise me.

I kept myself to myself for pretty much the rest of the day, don't worry, I don't become some kind of hermit, I just decided that I wanted to be alone. I gave Mel a call, and spoke to her, which always gave me a smile and made things seem cheery. Obviously not about what I'd done but the other things, leaving out that I had returned to the scene of the crime.

By the time I was in bed and trying to get some sleep, I had even formulated a plan to overcome what had happened and to try and stop any further niggles for the foreseeable future. I could only hope that I would continue to remain the elusive murderer that I would be jail free, and would be able to see out what I had in mind.

Lets face it, it was for the good of some other poor soul that I was trying to stay niggle free, its difficult to account for my actions when that niggle sets in, so I wanted to try and avoid it for as long as possible.

I decided that I would see about getting on with the plan the very next day, sleep wasn't long in coming.

THIRTY NINE

Now I'm able to look back at myself, and see how things were
back then, I can see that things were actually really good for me.
I mean, at the time I couldn't really see it, and there was a
considerable amount of thought that I would at any moment be
caught, but I can see now what a good time I should have been
having instead.

I had a beautiful girlfriend and we loved each other dearly, I had
just got a promotion at work, had a place of my own and a
decent car. There were a lot of things in my favour.

Of course there was the guilt starting to pile up, which would
every now and then sneak up on me and take me from the
thoughts of my normal life to those thoughts of, well, a
murderer.

All in all things were good, but I didn't fully realise it, despite
this, I did carry on with my life and carry on is just where we
were at, so excuse the meandering diversion, and I'll carry on
with the rest of what happened.

Like I was saying I had a plan, and as with things in the past, the
plan involved Mel. I'm not saying that Mel was just simply a
diversion, I was in love with her.

So when I saw her the following day, I asked her something that
I was hoping would change our lives together and would keep
that niggle in the back of my mind at bay.

We didn't do anything special, Mel came around to mine and we
rented a DVD from Blockbuster. Again, I don't know what the
film was, but before it started I asked Mel if we should start to
look for a place where we could live together.

Mel was excited, she was over the moon about the whole idea.
In fact while the DVD was playing in the machine, Mel was

flicking through a news paper looking at houses, she was asking what kind of area we should be looking to live.

By the end of the film we had narrowed the areas down, and I use the work 'we' in the loosest of terms, it was mainly Mel, we even had a kind of budget, judging by how much we were both earning. I have to say, it was quite exciting.

Within the following few days we had arranged to see a place, which although was not a million miles away from where my place was, it was in a much nicer location and a little bigger.

On the day we met up with the estate agent who showed us around the house; now I've seen daytime TV programs about nice little ways to sell your house, especially if it's been on the market for a while, little things like neutral colours and tidiness. The owners of the place we were looking at though clearly had not seen these programs.

I'm not the neatest of people, but to be honest the décor and complete untidiness in which the house, not to mention the garden was left put us both right off the idea. Neither of us could imagine even making a cup of tea in the kitchen or using the bathroom.

The first house that we saw didn't put us off the idea of moving though, and it wasn't long before we were viewing other places.

We must have viewed at least six properties, all in similar areas with similar prices, the estate agent would show us around, or the occupier would if they were available. We soon came to the conclusion that the areas where we were looking were not right for us.

In comparison to what I already had, the difference in price, size and location wasn't significant enough for us to want to move there. We decided to turn our attention to somewhere completely different, and to be honest, I'm glad we did.

FORTY

There's no need for me to go into all of the detail about the different places that we looked at, all the pros and cons that we considered, and all the haggling and negotiation that went on with the vendors and eventually our own solicitors (what an absolute bunch of assholes they are). I'm sure that you have done it yourself; and if not, you still have that to come and good luck for when you do!

As you can imagine all of this was occupying my mind, and taking up some time; I mean from the time that we decided to look for a place, to when we had agreed a price and things were starting to trundle along with the damned solicitors, it must have been six months or so.

Now obviously, things weren't so easy to start with, I mean I didn't just become involved in the move and forgot about the things that I had done, it didn't work like that. However as the weeks progressed I thought about things less and less.

I don't think there's a time when I don't think about those things, the terrible things I've done, but I try to keep the guilt about it at bay, hence the occupying of my mind. If I ever let the guilt take hold of me, I don't know what I'd do.

Now, the place that we found.

We decided to move attention to a different area, and we settled on an area just outside Bromsgrove. It wasn't far from the major M5 or M42 junction, so it was easy to get to work; and just 5 minutes away there was fields, which suited us just fine.

The place we settled on wasn't any bigger than we already had, it may have even been a tiny bit smaller, but it was a cottage, not a terraced house or a semi detached, but a cottage. We both loved the idea.

Mel had been excited when we had seen it, and I could tell from when we were walking around and how the place felt when we were there, that Mel really liked it. I felt comfortable there, which is a big thing for a man with my condition.

It was decided not long after we saw it that this was the place, and we decided that as long as it didn't break us we would have it. Neither of us wanted to pay as much as they wanted for it, but if we had to we would. As luck would have it, our first offer of five grand less than the asking price was accepted. Hoorah!

Like I say, I'd say the process then of getting things moving along towards the point of us getting a moving date, must have been six months or so from when we decided to start looking, but it was here and we were soon finding ourselves packing things away into boxes.

In the meantime, work was also going well, my promotion had developed and I was settling in nicely into the new role. Their was a lot of different things to get accustomed to, but it all added to the process of putting things clear in my mind, and keeping that niggle away from the forefront of my thoughts. The added benefit of the promotion was that it had given us that extra leeway on the funds, but it was too much of a pressured job that it was all consuming and Mel was left to sort everything out.

Now, perhaps most people would've panicked, and perhaps under different circumstances, it may have been me that was panic stricken, but I had just spent a decent amount of time putting things in order in my mind; so when it happened, I'm not saying I was ready, but I was at least not panicked by it.

FORTY ONE

I'll come back to the fact I didn't panic later, first I need to tell you about the move, as it was at the new house where things unfolded.

It was fraught, the day of the move was held up by the same money grabbing, time consuming, filled with self-importance solicitors that had dragged the ordeal out already.

It's an antiquated system that needs overhauling; the entire house buying procedure is languishing in the last century, and despite some things being computerised, in the main it's an outdated and unnecessary practice. Bringing value to a service that is worthless. You can keep your due diligence, I can work most things out for myself thank you.

I mean, why pay £200 to see if the house is supplied with gas and electric? I visited the house before I said I wanted to buy it. I physically actually saw that there was gas and electric. Anyway, I'm getting lost in my annoyance, I'll get back to it.

The phone call from the solicitor saying that contracts had been exchanged was a wonderful piece of news, especially after just an hour before they had said that the deal was unlikely to go through that day; which had bought an end to us packing up the last few things into a hired van, and had us sitting on the stairs waiting.

I don't know where the final push had come from, but in that moment all of my forlorn and demeaning ideas of conveyancing were pushed aside to ones of complete adoration; the complaint letter I had promised to send all but forgotten.

Mel and I packed the last few things into the van and we were off to the estate agent to leave my current keys and collect our new ones. We left a bottle of wine in the kitchen for the new owner of my old house.

Being in the van and pulling up outside our new home for the first time was fantastic, I looked over to Mel, pointed to it, and said that it was ours. It's amazing how the little words make a difference, ours, instead of mine, I was over the moon.

The important things went into the house, first, we had kept these separate from the rest as we knew we couldn't live without them. The kettle, two cups and some tea bags.

Don't worry, I'd organised the broadband, but that was still two weeks away.

We sat on the floor in the living room of our new home; the conservatory overlooked a decent rear garden that backed onto nothing but fields. I felt a tranquil and content feeling flood over me as I sat there with Mel enjoying a nice hot cup of tea in our home.

The feeling doesn't last for long though, like I say there's something not too far around the corner, but for now, for right now, let me just enjoy that feeling again.

Mel was relentless.

I hadn't really seen that side of her, but she worked without a break to get the furniture in the right place, to have furniture built and to have our little cottage ready for us to live in. I mean, it was only three days after getting the keys, and there were only a few boxes left unopened in the garage.

FORTY TWO

No, don't be absurd.

There is absolutely no way whatsoever that Mel has discovered any of my murderous ways, Mel is a lovely person, and if ever she had ever discovered about the terrible things I have done, I would have been in jail a long time ago.

This was a news report, not a breaking news report, like passenger jets have been flown into the twin towers, just a local news report about a police collaboration, but an important one.

The news report detailed how a Scottish murder investigation had been tied to three murders that had taken place in the wider Midlands area; three police forces were involved and were joining forces to catch a potential serial killer. Obviously they didn't actually say there was a serial killer on the loose.

The news report included a photograph of me.

It was the still capture from the CCTV of me in the hotel in Glasgow and now all three police forces were wanting to speak to the person from the photograph, to eliminate him from their enquiries.

They said that someone other than the person photographed should surely know who that person was and to come forward with information.

Now, I had been in this position before, and I had the tried and tested method of keeping quiet as my ally. I had also pushed murder so far to the back of my mind, that when it came to the forefront, it wasn't like the ice bucket challenge dowsing in freezing water, but a quiet contemplation of what it meant.

A few things ran through my mind to start with, and that was, the photograph was not very clear. Let's face it, I'm Mr Average. I'm average height and build, with short dark hair, and no distinguishing features. My general description, the kind of description that the police get to work with could realistically describe about twenty five percent of the people in my office block.

Please don't take what I am saying as any kind of arrogance, that I may have thought that there was no chance of being caught, because that couldn't be further from the truth. This news report made me positively uneasy, but I could cope.

With everything that was going on in my life, with Mel and the house, it made my ability to cope with this revelation a little easier.

Still, I found myself sitting in a chair, staring at a TV that had turned itself off, with a cold cup of tea in my hand after I first saw the report.

Who knows what time it was when I actually went to bed, suffice to say that when my alarm went off for work, I could have cried; I wanted to turn over and ignore it, but knew deep down that in five minutes time I'd be up and in the shower.

When I got into work, there were a few employees who had made it in before me, we exchanged the normal greetings and I made my way to my office.

Now the office as a whole was pretty much open plan; the place that I called my office was one in a line of three rooms that were situated on the far wall of the main office floor, these rooms were the only part of the floor that was segregated properly; with stud walls and glass fronted. There was the option to close the office door should the need arise, but this was very are.

There was a moment of shock when I reached my closed office door, there was an A4 piece of paper Selotaped to the glass. On that piece of A4 paper was a print out from the BBC website, which included the photograph of a murderer. This murderer looked surprisingly like me.

I had to consider my response to this poster very carefully, I mean, if I took this the wrong way, there was the possibility I could be ousted, right here today.

I had to consider that this was a joke, a practical joke by people who wrongly assumed that this person from the CCTV looked a lot like me, but there was no way that it could actually be me. If it had been anything other than a joke, it would have been a secret call to Crimestoppers instead.

If you recall I had worked in this office for quite a while, I mean I used to work at the same desk as some of the people in the office right now, and you can't work closely with each other without there being some banter between people, and this poster was nothing more than that.

They knew that I would take it light heartedly and probably make a joke of it, and if that was what they would probably expect, then that was what I needed to do.

FORTY THREE

The workplace is a contrived and duplicitous place, I worked
with the same people day in and day out. I knew their names,
their daughters/sons and wives names and the kind of things they
liked to do when they weren't at work. We got along, we joked,
we were serious at times and we spent the majority of our
waking time together.

In reality though we were mostly feathering our own careers;
and if I could take credit for someone else's good work behind
their back, so be it. We lied to each other about how successful
we were, how nice our houses were and how good our cars were
to drive. We chatted how perfect our family lives were, when
often things couldn't be further from the truth.

We were all liars, some little white lies and in my case huge
fully grown deep black overbearing lies; liars all the same.

Anyway, being two faced was a primal part of being in the
workplace, and that suited me just fine, I was the poker king, no-
one knew what I was capable of or had done; I revelled in the
fact I was such a stranger to these people.

So, I sent the four closest workmates an email about a meeting,
and scheduled it for 11:00, I knew it would've been one of this
four who would be responsible for the poster.

When they arrived in my office, each was clutching either a
notepad or book and were armed with a pen. As they entered I
walked behind them and closed the door, a serious look pasted
on my face and projected an air of concern. The door being
closed emphasised that this was a discreet meeting.

I sat down at my desk and looked up, I hadn't said a word, and
had caught them looking at each other with an awkward look
that said 'what the fuck is going on.'

I explained that the poster had been seized and was with higher management who were looking into it, that they considered such an obtuse and disturbing attempt at jest to be totally inappropriate and considered it as a case of gross misconduct; someone was going to get the sack.

I said I needed an email from each of them by 12:00 naming or admitting so I could take it and discuss the matter with higher management; I explained that I would try and resolve it without the need for formal proceedings. I dismissed them from my office.

As they sheepishly left the office, I closed the office door behind them, I returned to my desk and picked up the phone. There was no-one on the other end, and I wasn't going to call anyone myself, it just added to the effect if anyone looked back; but they didn't.

It didn't take until 12:00 to receive the emails, and clearly they had spoken about the matter before sending them. Jack admitted he was responsible for the poster, and the others named him. I was glad, as it was Jack that I was probably closest to, which is probably why he had felt comfortable enough with the gag in the first place.

A few minutes after I received the emails I called Jack into the office and closed the door.

As I sat at my desk I said how funny the poster was, I kept a stony look on my face while talking to him in case anyone was trying to see through the glass frontage into the office. I admitted that no one was upset by the poster, there was no management involved, but said we should continue the prank together.

I took Jack out for a coffee in the canteen, but as we left the office into the lift, Jack turned and gave his colleagues a concerned look, the lift could be taking us upstairs to management, but it wasn't, we went down to the canteen.

Free from the office we joked about the poster, and how I could see the resemblance. How horrific the murders were and what a psycho the guy must be. He must be a loner, no friends, no family sitting in a dingy flat somewhere like a recluse. We painted a dirty, solitary, lonely and desperate life for the guy in the picture; a life that in no way matched my own, it was a win win. I reinforced the picture Jack and clearly others would have about this person's life, and gave it credence like I was thinking exactly the same.

I was actually thinking about choking him to death with his own tie.

When we returned to the office I accompanied Jack to his desk, he was looking forlorn as we agreed, there was a look of abject concern from the others, when we started sniggering our game was up and we came clean about the entire thing.

I would like to think that engineering the situation and them in this way, made me to be the killer even more improbable. In any case, no-one mentioned it again.

FORTY FOUR

I arrived back home with a banging headache which was causing me a little annoyance, Mel wouldn't be home until later, so I started on some dinner for us. I took a couple of painkillers and set about making some food.

When Mel returned home she was greeted with a warm hug and the smell of home cooked food, I could see she immediately relaxed, as she took off her shoes, we held each other for a moment, then she went upstairs to get out of her office clothes.

By the time she came downstairs, dinner was out and as I heard her approach started to fill a glass with red wine, everything was ready for her to sit down and enjoy.

We talked about our day, I failed to mention anything about the poster, I did not want that kind of suspicion from Mel.

I'm sure you know already, Mel never finds out, and in a way, that's one thing I'm glad of.

We spent the rest of the evening in my favourite position, cuddled up on the sofa watching the TV; I can't remember if there was a film on or just catching up, but the chores were put off to another time, as chores always should be. Life is for the living, you never know what is around the corner, and I of all people should know that.

Anyway, despite recent events at work I was feeling pretty tranquil and relaxed. The little game I had played with my co-workers had helped in keeping the panic, the guilt and thoughts of what I had done at bay; allowing me to enjoy this time with Mel.

I looked at her while she wasn't watching and took note of her face, the way her hair fell, the shape of her lips and nose, a look of contented happiness on her face. It made me happy in myself.

As I sat there comfortable and relaxed I drifted off to sleep, Mel nestled against me, it felt perfect and looking back I would say that this was the happiest I had been.

I mean, putting aside the murders for a moment, I was kind of living the dream.

Cuddled up with a beautiful woman in my arms, sleeping on the sofa in a handsome little cottage that we have bought together. We have a lovely home, nice cars each and disposable income that we can use on pretty much anything that we want. All in all it's a pretty splendid existence, and that's not talking in a workplace environment kind of way, no arrogance or bragging. Just an honest appraisal of how life was for me back then.

This is a picture postcard memory that I often return to; it's funny to think how things change. How quickly they change sometimes and at other times things change right before your eyes and you don't see it.

Well there are some big changes a foot, and I'll tell you all about that soon enough, but for now let me just revel in this precious moment a little while longer.

FORTY FIVE

The scream that woke us both up was coming out of my mouth.

In the quietness of early morning, as it was just about to strike 1am; the scream pierced the stillness like a chainsaw, it resonated off the walls and it seemed to echo in our ears that had become accustomed to the quiet.

It was a fight or flight reaction from Mel who leaped off the sofa like a ninja, she was staring back at me with wide eyes and shaking a little.

My mouth remained open for a moment or two, despite the scream having ended as I woke up. For me there was a moment as to whether there had actually been a scream at all, and whether the echo in my ears was all part of a dream.

Looking at Mel gave me the answer.

Neither of us knew what to say, Mel broke the rediscovered silence by breaking down into laughter. It was that instantly contagious kind of laughter and I immediately started laughing too.

She collapsed back into our cuddle, still laughing. She couldn't believe how loud I screamed, and how much it had scared us. She actually swore, which was a rarity in itself and gave me a playful smack against my shoulder.

I worried straight away.

Nothing like this had ever happened to me before, it was completely new. I'd coped with what I had done in my own way, I wasn't expecting anything like this. I wasn't sure it was directly linked to anything I had done, but surely people don't just scream out loud for no reason.

I may have been over thinking things, it may have been an

overreaction, but that moment, when I screamed out loud and scared the love of my life half to death I wondered. I wondered what else I could be capable of doing without knowing it.

I mean, what if I got lost in a memory when sleeping and ended up hurting Mel? What if something worse happened, how could I live with myself.

This thought made me apprehensive about going to sleep, when we went to bed I lay awake for what seemed like an age, worrying about something happening. When I finally drifted off I had scuttled as far away from Mel as I could, I was lying on my side taking up around 6 inches of the bed, facing away from her.

When I awoke she was cuddling me, still very much alive. I felt a flood of relief wash over me.

Don't worry, I didn't get carried away by this, this doesn't cause a rift between us or have any real bearing in what happens to us; I just wanted to bring it up, as it seemed strange after everything I'd done and would do that this simple occurrence caused me so much consternation.

I'll tell you though, for the next few nights, probably into a week or so afterwards, I was concerned, and had difficulty sleeping. After this though I settled back down and recovered my comfort, normality resumed and after a short time I thought nothing of it at all; until it happened again.

It doesn't happen yet, and I'll come back to that later, there's a lot that goes on in between now and then that we need to cover first, suffice to say that the first scream was not the last, and things get rather complicated from here on in. Even if you thought things were complicated enough already.

FORTY SIX

If any of you had known me, I don't mean if you knew me to wave to in the street; I mean if you had known me closely like my brother, my dad etc, you would know there's one thing I'd always wanted.

OK, I mean I have always wanted a TVR, there's just something about them I like, I remember I came very close to buying a Chimera one year; I know they break down often and aren't a reliable drive to work every day car (which is probably why I didn't end up buying it), but that sound and the turn of speed is electrifying.

No, something else, and I'll come to it shortly.

Some people say that there are no such things as coincidences, and that every person that comes into your life happens for a reason, to either pass you a message, show you something or to remain in your life by your side loving you.

I'm not sure myself, but I have noticed that there are some coincidences that strike you as being odd; the number of times I have said to someone that I was just thinking the very thing that they had said is passed counting.

My dad used to say that no good deed goes unpunished, and we were often able to attribute a spot of bad luck that followed a moment of good will or help towards someone else.

I've also bore witness to the opposite though too, when you do something nice and without even knowing it someone else has done something nice for you.

You probably think I don't deserve nice things happening to me, well they do; so if that ruins your concept of the yin bringing the yang back into unity or karma having its way, then I'm sorry, but nice things do happen to me, and my family and friends love me.

145

So, coincidences, you'll see what I mean soon enough how this all ties together.

I was at work and hadn't been doing anything in particular, the prank wasn't spoken about again, and there was nothing further from any of my colleagues other than the usual chat. There was a couple of things that I needed to do, but I decided that I could put them off until tomorrow, instead I closed my office a little early and used some flexi-time to get out of there.

On the way out I checked my watch to make sure that I had enough time to do what I wanted to do, I got into my car and headed into the town centre.

You've probably guessed it, I wanted to make a nice meal and buy some flowers for Mel, just completely out of the blue, as I wanted her to know that she was always on my mind and that I loved her. For no other reason than being her, not because it was an anniversary, or birthday or other special event; just a normal day; I loved her and appreciated her.

I stopped off first at the florist and put my order in, so that they could put the bouquet together while I shopped for the food. Lilies were a must, everything else could be patched in, I was not even that bothered about roses, there had to be Lilies though.

Is steak the go to celebratory meal food for everyone (vegetarians aside)? Well, it was for us, Mel even liked a rare steak. I always enjoyed my steak rare too, and it was sometimes hard to find a place who would risk the rare cooking of a decent steak.

I didn't put my faith in Asda or Tesco for the steak, instead I went to an actual butcher and bought my from them, it wasn't really any more expensive and I think the meat from the butcher is better.

Anyway, the rest of the stuff I got from Asda and obviously some stuff I already had, so required no extra shopping at all.

146

By the time I was done and popped back to the florists, the bouquet was ready for me; I chose a card and wrote a little message and put the card in an envelope; the florist put the card in a special little card holder in amongst the flowers. I was pleased with the look of the flowers.

I was excited, I loved doing this kind of thing a whole lot more than suffocating someone to death, and although I was holding a white plastic bag with blood collecting at the bottom and holding in the folds from the tie at the top, I didn't see any analogy. I was too focused on what lay ahead, which as it turns out was not entirely what I had in mind.

FORTY SEVEN

The drive home was uncomplicated and as I landed onto the driveway outside our little cottage I was met with a surprise of my own.

Mel was already home.

I usually made it home well before Mel so that I was able to get dinner at least part way cooked before she got in; it was our kind of thing, Mel was a reluctant chef where as I quite enjoyed it. Mel usually tidied up, there was a slight element of OCD about her, and even if I'd clean up after cooking, she would have to go over things herself. Hence she asked me to leave it whenever I tried to give a hand, it saved her time.

Anyway, seeing the car on the driveway gave me a pang of uncertainty. She hadn't said she was finishing early, there was no reason for her to be home already. A million questions raced through my mind, was everything OK; was she ill, had something happened at work.

I left what I had bought at the shops in the car, worried at why she was home so early and went to the front door. Her key was in the other side and I was unable to unlock it and let myself in. I started to feel a little more apprehension about what was going on.

I gave the bell to the side of the door a push and heard the melody ring from inside, for good measure I also gave the door a hearty knock.

I saw movement out of the corner of my eye and turned to see Mel appear at the front window in her dressing gown looking out to who would be at the door before opening it.

I saw her leave the window and head towards the door, through the frosted glass in the front door I saw her readjusting her dressing gown as she approached the door, it unlocked and she opened it or me.

She stood there looking sheepish, as if she had been found out, as if I had caught her in the act. She brushed her hair from the side of her face and for a moment stood there not knowing what to do, before standing aside and letting me in.

My apprehension had turned into concern and there was a turbulent feeling in my stomach as to what I was going to find and what Mel was going to say.

My heart was kind of in my mouth, these thoughts and feelings being processed in the seconds it took to walk past her and into the hallway and then turn round to speak to her.

As I turned she had her back towards me as she was closing the front door and making sure it was locked behind us; another of her slight OCD features was security, knowing that the door was locked was important to her, which is why I was unsurprised to see her come to the window first without blindly opening the door.

When Mel turned back towards me she still portrayed a sheepish look in her body language, she averted from my gaze and had one arm crossed across her body keeping the opening of her dressing gown closed, the other hand idly sweeping her hair back off her face.

She looked as though she expected to be in trouble, or that she was about to deliver some devastating bad news and didn't know how to start the conversation.

It was me who spoke first.

FORTY EIGHT

I'll come back to all that in a minute, I just need to clarify a couple of things.

Now, I've said it a couple of times about the slight OCD that Mel has. For those who don't know OCD is Obsessive Compulsive Disorder that affects many people in many different ways and degrees. A little like the autistic spectrum.

Mel, if she actually has OCD has a very mild version. For example she does not have to have the stickers of the tins of food in the cupboards all facing out. The cup handles don't have to be at 90 degrees from the table edge, any of that kind of stuff, I'd actually say she is particular as opposed to having OCD.

For example we've spoken about cleaning up the kitchen and the door locks, but she will often rub her finger over the light switch a number of times, just to make sure it remains in the off position throughout the night. Likewise with the power sockets, they all have to be off (she accepts the broadband is an exception), so that nothing can spontaneously combust while we sleep.

I think it is these things and the acceptance of them that make a relationship work, I've never really taken the piss out of her, ok, I sometimes remark on her level of having OCD, but she knows that this is just a friendly jest and not a malicious jibe.

I'm sure I have some traits that she would point out to you as being unusual or funny, but she never makes an issue out of my foibles either; and therein I think lies a degree of contentment and happiness. It says to her that accept you for who you are and she returns the compliment to me, without the need for either of us actually to say anything to each other.

I think this is a dying art in relationships, people are all too ready to point out the differences in others, instead of accepting and understanding.

Does any of this have any bearing on my murderous ways? Does it make you feel any differently about me? Could you accept what I had done and move forward with me, treat as the normal person that I am?

I'll leave that with you to ponder.

Anyway, what I'm trying to say is that Mel and I are pretty confident in our feelings for each other, in such a way that it often doesn't need expressing verbally. I'm not having to constantly reassure her of my love or the way I feel about her. Likewise she doesn't have to reassure me.

Sure, there are times when a little reassurance is needed, as with everything, but it isn't a constant thing, I think the constant reassurance of feelings is so draining on people that relationships of this kind cannot last long.

So, with those feelings comes the trust, I trust Mel, and she trusts me. I know what you're going to say that how can she trust me when she doesn't know me; but she does know me, in all the ways that two people know each other.

Let's not pretend there are no dark secrets between you and your lover/partner. So, they may not be as dark as my secrets, but look inside yourself, do they actually know the full you? All the things good and bad that you've done, your secret desires fantasies or fetishes.

Are you truly fully open without a single thing to hide? If not we are not too dissimilar you and I, and the thought we are somehow alike must scare you, how far away from me you are is an answer only you know, but let that answer niggle in your mind, in a not to dissimilar way I have a niggle in mine.

FORTY NINE

I remember asking if everything was OK, with a kind of weird apprehensive feeling on what the answer was likely to be.

Her answer didn't really explain anything at all, she was somewhat vague and elusive, we were talking as we walked towards the kitchen, and in the kitchen I saw that Mel had been preparing a meal, there were potatoes in the sink waiting to be peeled and a pot of water on the work surface, awaiting those freshly peeled spuds.

Mel went on to say that she wasn't expecting me back for a while, and started to question why I had finished work early.

In a shift of questioning I became elusive and evasive and probably seemed a little vague, and said that I needed to go back to my car first.

I think she looked as perplexed as I felt.

I went back out to the car and picked up the shopping and the bouquet, as I turned I saw that Mel had followed and although she was a few steps back, so as not to be obvious, she was looking out of the window at what I was doing. I noticed that as I turned and exposed the bouquet, she left the front room and returned to the kitchen.

When I returned to the hallway and used my foot to close the front door, Mel appeared in the doorway to the kitchen, she was smiling and did give me a look of surprise at seeing the bouquet, but I knew that she had already seen the flowers.

She came over to me and ignoring the flowers, gave me a long hug, I wanted to hold her back, but my hands were full of food and flowers. She kissed me on the side of my face and neck, on the side that was nearest, then she took the flowers from me and almost skipped into the kitchen.

Seeing her excited and happy, made me feel great, it was such a warm feeling, it put a smile on my face. I followed her into the kitchen. Mel was already kneeling down looking in one of the cupboards for the vase.

Now this is what I meant a while ago about coincidences, you'll see more what I mean in a little while, it's worth the wait though, I promise.

So we continued talking while Mel arranged the flowers into the vase, remembering the little sachet of additive for the water to keep them fresh for longer, both of really forgetting that either was home early until the flowers were ready and set on the windowsill in the front room.

I explained to Mel my thoughts for the day, and that I had wanted to come home and surprise her with a meal, just to say that I loved her every day and appreciated everything she did for me. How much I was grateful for our relationship and how happy she made me.

Mel was so excited, she gave me the biggest hug, almost leaping into my arms and wrapping her legs around my waist, I took a couple of steps back taking the momentum of her jump, then steadied myself and hugged her too.

All apprehension, all wonder and worry had left me; Mel was clearly not unwell, her gymnastic prowess showed me that, she hadn't appeared ill or upset, and these were the things that had bothered me.

Mel loosened her grip with her legs allowing me to hold her against me, her feet dangling from the floor, until I gently placed her back down. She let go of her arms around my neck, and gave me a fleeting glance in my eyes, an almost imperceivable glance it was so quick before looking for and taking hold of my hand. She led me upstairs.

Now at this point, I usually say something along the lines of three is a crowd and you'll have to just imagine what goes on next, but not this time, not this time at all.

So, Mel leads me upstairs and instead of going to the bedroom, she leads me into the bathroom, now she has her bath robe on, but the bath is empty and the shower hasn't been running.

In the bathroom we have a small vanity closet beneath the sink, meaning that the sink is encased in what is a small work surface in essence; we keep a bottle of hand wash and cup containing the toothbrushes there.

Sitting around the sink there are three pieces of plastic and a cardboard box, the box says 'clearblue' on it. I'm no fool, I know what these pieces of plastic are, and as I pick up each pregnancy test, I see that each one says 'pregnant'.

I was going to be a dad.

FIFTY

If I could have leaped into Mel's arms I would have, instead I took her in my arms and placed my right hand on her tummy as I kissed her. I could have held her this way infinitum, I closed my eyes and took in the gravity of what this meant.

It was a moment that will last with me forever; the feel of strands of her hair against my cheek, the softness of her skin against mine, the smell of her perfume filling my senses enhancing them somehow, the feel of her body against my arms and her tummy against the palm of my hand. An intoxicating mix of sensation and emotion that forms such a vivid memory that it is ingrained into the brain. It is a moment that although fleeting in reality, lasts a lifetime through my thoughts.

Probably my next thought, somewhat selfishly, was that I was very pleased that my balls worked; a very strange thought to have hearing the news that I was going to be a dad, all the same, there it was.

Now you would think that how my life is unfolding would be the end of the necessity for any further murder, but you're wrong, so very wrong.

I had been thinking about slyly killing one of my colleagues for a while, not really any of the ones I liked at work, just someone else from the same workplace, and not anyone in particular, just whoever happened to be in the wrong place at the wrong time.

It hadn't developed into the niggle that needed scratching yet, but I had become aware of it, nothing major just an inkling now and then.

How can I think of murder at a time like this you ask? I have just been told that I'm going to be a dad and that my beautiful girlfriend is pregnant. You're right, and remember I said earlier about there being one thing I'd always wanted (not the TVR), well this was it, I had dreamed of being a dad from when I was in my teens.

You'd think that this would be exactly the kind of thing that would keep the niggle at bay, like so many similar things before. Not this time, this news was a kind of a flip flop of the usual response, it bought murder more to the front of my mind than it had been for a long time.

I was soon to embark on a journey of nurturing the most precious and vulnerable thing I could ever have imagined. To care for, protect and raise a child of my own. I had to make sure that this desire to murder was done before the arrival; I want to be a role model.

Besides, one in, one out is how the saying goes isn't it?

I can't begin to tell you how over the moon I was knowing I was going to be a dad; it's not like we were trying to have a baby, but we weren't trying not to have a baby if that makes sense.

I had never been in a better position to bring a new someone into the world, well we both had good jobs, obviously there was my promotion and the little cottage we'd bought. So it just seemed natural that this would be the next step.

I couldn't wait to see my parent's faces when we told them, my brother's either.

So, exciting times afoot, I have my family to tell the good news to and someone I have to kill; again the latter I need to think about so as I'm not behind bars when the baby arrives. I've found I have a knack for this though, so leave it with me for a little while, I'll let you know my plans.

Let's not forget where we are though, Mel is the important one in this equation, she is now in possession of precious cargo; with all of the commotion and excitement, and despite the early finishes for both of us, neither of us has got around to making dinner. As it happens Mel bought steak too.

There it is you see, the coincidence, for no reason at all I finished work early, only there was a reason, a reason I knew nothing about, which bought me home for this special moment. To share in this moment with Mel and revel in this extra time we had together that neither of us would usually have.

See, I'm still not too sure about the coincidences thing, but you have to admit, this particular example is pretty good, is it a coincidence we both finished work early and prepared a surprise for each other, or is it a cosmic plan, that is laid out that we follow?

Despite being very excited, I forwent the urge to give my parents a call and blurt out the news, I knew how excited they'd be too, instead I wanted to tell them in another way, so I left the phone alone and ordered a couple of things from my trusty internet, with next day delivery.

Seeing as we were both now past preparing a meal for the other, and considering this was a really good news day, we decided to order in some food.

So we ordered ourselves some Indian food for delivery, and I treated myself to a beer or two; wine was now off the agenda for Mel.

We cosied down for the night, and looking back now at this, I can't remember a more content feeling.

FIFTY ONE

To say that I awoke on cloud nine would be an understatement.
The alarm had gone off as usual, forcing me out of my dream
against my will in order that I get ready to go to work.

I was too happy to go to work though, I mean, I was going to be
a dad, so I decided to turn the alarm off and snuggle up to Mel, a
little longer. I'd wait until people started arriving at work and
would call in ill. I'd throw what people call a sickie.

There was an extra special content kind of feeling, as I lay in bed
for longer than I should, knowing that my colleagues would be
going into work and toiling for another day, leaving me at home
enjoying myself, snug beneath the duvet hugging my beautiful
girlfriend.

I popped down to the local shop, and picked up bacon, we had
eggs but decided I'd make at least a kind of breakfast sandwich
for us seeing as Mel decided not to go into work either; she was
such a rebel.

It was going to be a bit of a pyjama day, I had briefly dressed
into my jeans to go to the shop, but once back my pj's were back
on, this needed to be a relaxing and enjoyable day where there
was no pressure on either of us and we could just chill out
together.

We talked about telling out parents, and we came to the
conclusion that we would wait until the 20 week scan to let
anyone know. That way we would know that everything was
fine and appeared normal before passing out the news, so for the
time being it was our little secret. I'm used to secrets.

I had the bacon in the pan, we both liked it well done and crispy,
so I'd left the eggs for a while; I heated up a pan and used a
knife to crack open the egg. As the knife came down and the
egg shell split open, the sound that came with it was a low thud,
the inside of the egg exposed through a line of broken outer

shell.

Emma Jackson's fractured skull came to mind, that sound, although only vaguely similar to the hammer, as it cracked open her skull seemed to resonate through me. I stood there for a second, blood dripping from the claw hammer and Emma's empty eyes looking at me as I held the split egg in my hands.

I pulled the egg apart and the yolk and white sizzled into the hot pan.

I don't know if I'd ever had a flashback like it, I can't recall so, but that image linked to the sound that conjured itself up into my mind's eye, well, that was something I needed to try to avoid, I didn't need that horrible shit coming back to haunt me, especially not at fun family times like these.

I needed to do something, as the eggs and bacon cooked, I realised how quickly I needed to do something to sort myself out; I couldn't lapse into the state where I was conjuring up images like this, it would interfere massively with my life and the plan that revolved around being happy and not behind bars.

I knew what the answer was, and it meant that someone else had to die, but I needed to keep myself together, and that was worth at least one more life.

This was an important time for me, I needed to be clear, I didn't want any distractions and it was a necessity to be ready for when the baby arrived, Mel would expect nothing less from me, and I wouldn't expect to give less than 100% in getting ready for the birth.

So I had a very strict timeline, I needed to work something out and execute it (if you pardon the pun) within a short timeframe if I was going to be ready for the little one to come along.

The egg was slightly over cooked, but the bacon was perfect.

FIFTY TWO

I'd like to say that it was easy to figure it all out, but it wasn't. I mean there was a couple of things I had to throw into the mix.

I had an idea about what I wanted to do, but doing it one particular way could end up being quite incriminating, especially if you link it all up with everything else that I've done, the CCTV and the ongoing police investigation.

I'll tell you the plan later, but I needed to break from what I was used to if I was going to pull it off.

There was still no identifiable target in mind and it would again be a case of wrong place wrong time for the victim, but I always thought that that was best.

Let's face it, in things like this, people are always trying to identify a motive; money, sex, property, greed or betrayal. People always think that there is some kind of gain linked to the murder, pecuniary or otherwise.

No-one is ever going to believe that someone died because of a cracked egg, but there it is.

So let's talk plan, like I said earlier one way could be incredibly incriminating, and that would be what I'd been thinking about ages ago and to top one of my work colleagues.

If you add in the prank that had already been played on me, I soon came to the decision that I had to keep my murder out of the workplace; sure there were at least a couple of people there I'd be happy to knock off, but I was also sure as eggs that that would lead to my arrest.

That part of the plan, my arrest, simply could not happen.

With my thinking cap on, I found myself working out shrewd ways of killing someone; I mean, in those moments of solace, sitting on the toilet, waiting in the darkness for sleep, driving around and sometimes while mindless TV programs were blurting in the corner of the room, this is when I conjured up my plan.

I've said it before and I'll say it again, the internet is amazing thing, and as time progressed so has the power of the internet.

Honestly, with how fast things like online shopping of grown and the availability of everything online, along with it came far more stringent controls, not like before; I mean, I doubt I could still get away with ordering a taser like I did before, I had a feeling most things were tracked auditable and every click could be followed if needs be.

However, innocuous things were still available and I doubt all purchases were subject to the same level of security of a taser.

It was probably a good thing that good old taser was safely stored up my mom and dad's loft.

So I created myself a new email address under a fake name, and then used the address to create an eBay account under the same false name, Dave Johnson, don't know why, just two names that instantly popped into my head.

It took me a little while to work out the exact details, and what it should look like, but soon enough I'd placed an order via eBay, and ok, it would take a couple of weeks to arrive, but there was other stuff I needed to do, so the time scale fitted right in.

I decided I'd need a cheap old car, which I wasn't afraid to just abandon; So I got straight onto my newly founded eBay account for that too; I would also need a place to store it for a while, luckily I had a good idea for where that might be.

FIFTY THREE

Let's not forget, life goes on as normal. I mean I know I'd
thrown a sickie the day after I had found out I was going to be a
dad, but life carried on and I was still going to work and
enjoying life with Mel. My planning and thought about murder
had to go on in the background.

I know what you're thinking; you'd know. If it were you, you'd
know that something wasn't right and that I was up to
something, that you would have found out, somehow. That
there's absolutely no way something as big as this could be kept
from someone, and that there'd be warning signs.

Well you're wrong.

You haven't got a clue what is going on someone else's life;
they tell you what they do, they tell you what they think, but
you'll never actually know it, and unless you follow them every
minute, you'll never actually know where they are. Affairs
happen every day, often for years at a time, yet nothing is
challenged, there are no indicators.

My affair is murder, which is better than taking someone's love,
abusing it and cheating on them. I'm completely true to Mel; she
can trust me with her love.

Anyway, the plan is already in motion, and I have scoped out a
couple of cars that I'm looking to buy, this time I can't recruit
Chris to help, this time I have to go and work it out on my own, I
don't want to turn him into an accomplice.

So, there's a guy up in Cheshire in a place called Winsford who
has an older 5 series BMW up for sale, it's the right price
judging by how much I have saved in my murder fund savings
account, and having spoken to him he sounds a little dodgy,
which is the right kind of thing for what I need.

I caught a train from Wolverhampton, which goes straight from one station to the other, and he said he'd meet me in the station car park with the car. After just over an hour on the train, we pulled into the station at Winsford, the train was going to carry on into Liverpool, this was my stop though.

Winsford station car park isn't very big, there's about 15 parking spaces, all of which were taken, and kind of bus parking bay to the side of the parking spaces; as I walked into the car park a little mini bus was pulling out of the parking bay, pulled past the front of the station and back out through the entrance/exit.

I thought Cheshire was meant to be nice; this was as dismal but much smaller as the station I'd come from.

I saw a dark blue 5 series BMW parked up just behind the bus parking bay, as there had clearly been no parking spaces left in the small car park. I approached it and the driver got out of the car. We introduced ourselves and I had a quick look at the bodywork.

There were quite a few little dents and scratches, but all in all, seeing as it was 12 years old the bodywork looked ok, and I thought with a bit of a polish it could look pretty good. Who am I kidding, I wasn't going to polish it; I was going to kill someone in it.

I asked him to start it up and was standing at the back to make sure there was no cloud of smoke, I asked him to rev it, no oil or anything came out of the exhaust, a good sign, I didn't want it breaking down on me with a body in the back; I was not prepared to do a 'Weekend at Bernies' type of sketch with a dead body.

I checked the normal things, no oil mixing with water in the oil cap, water level was good and that the oil seemed ok.

Then we went out for a test drive. This is where I really like BMW's, the drive was great, as good, if not better than my current car, which was a lot newer. It had plenty of power, and once away from the station I started to see some of that pleasant

163

Cheshire countryside, nice.

To be honest, the car drove better than I was expecting and all round it looked a decent car, well worth the £450 he was asking.

Now this is why I wanted someone a little dodgy, the car wasn't registered to him, he didn't have the full log book, but the little green slip for the new owner. He didn't ask me my name, or anything, and when the money changed hands he gave me the green slip, to send off to DVLA so I could get the car registered.

I wasn't going to register the car, this was perfect.

There was only one key and the remote locking didn't work, the doors all locked on the key though, and that was enough for me

I drove the car back towards home, straight down the M6 onto the M5 and parked it up in the place I'd found, we'll come to that place later.

Where had I been? To see Mouse for a while, It was a Saturday and it had taken me 3 hours all in, which was reasonable, when I arrived back into our little cottage, Mel didn't even consider I'd been anywhere else.

All I needed now was my delivery from eBay, my faithful roll of black electrical tape, and the right victim to come along.

I was ready.

FIFTY FOUR

Mel and I had been out walking one of the days, to be honest it probably wasn't too long after we had first moved in, and we had wanted to see what was around us. There's no better way than to discover a place than on foot. You see so much more than when you're driving, and although it's slower, if you're in the right company then its ok. I was in the right company.

We'd been walking about an hour and a half and neither of us really knew where we were or how to get back home; it was a bit of a laugh to be honest, feeling somewhat stranded but too proud to try and get any help.

It doesn't take long to be out in the countryside from where we are, so to find ourselves in the middle of nowhere with our only option to trace back our steps and find civilisation.

On the way back I found a gravel driveway, almost overgrown with trees and weeds. I had a rough idea on our direction and this was headed the same way, clearly a road that hadn't been used for some time, but might cut a while off our journey.

We trudged the pathway for a while, before it led neatly to a large detached house, the windows had been boarded, but it was double fronted with a large entrance door. It was a substantial building but in semi ruins.

Structurally everything looked intact, the roof although not perfect hadn't dropped and despite the wood on the windows, it was easy to see that it would make a lavish home. It was hard to understand how a building like this could reach the point it was in without someone caring for it.

Have you seen the film The Notebook?

This was instantly my thought, I needed to buy this house and restore it. Ok Mel and I were still together and it would not be in a bid to win her back, but it was the place I would like to be our forever home where we could bring children up.

I didn't say anything at the time, but as we walked around the grounds and then tried peeking through the gaps in the wood on the windows to see inside, I knew I wanted to buy it.

Don't get me wrong, I knew it would take a lot of fixing up, and cost a lot to renovate, but I thought it would be worth it, and an incredible property when refurbished.

I could tell Mel liked it too, and it was at this point I felt like Noah with Mel as my Allie; me ready to rebuild a house in the name of our love.

Obviously I didn't know how I was going to go about it, or even where to start, I just knew at some point I wanted to be living in that house with Mel.

Now at this point in my life, I didn't realise quite how much things were going to change, I kind of had a plan how I wanted things to work out and where I'd be, despite not having any concrete plans in place; it's amazing though how different life actually turns out to what you had figured, and how very little resembles the idea in your head at all.

Now this house is important, firstly it gives you more of an idea of how much I love Mel and the lengths I'm willing to go.

It also gives me a little known place, not overlooked to say, park a second car until I needed to use it, without it causing any suspicion to anyone at all.

If you are going to commit murder, little places like this are really important, and this was just what I would need.

FIFTY FIVE

So now you know where my new car was parked, ok, different car, it certainly wasn't new. With it being so secluded there, I was able to do the things I needed without being seen by anyone, which is always a bonus.

Ok, so this is why you're reading really, you want to know what happens next.

It was Saturday night, summer was on its way out, but the trees were still full of leaves, but they were on the change from luscious green, to developing a brown and orange tinge. Some leaves had fallen already, but most were still there, it was a picturesque time of year.

It wasn't particularly cold yet, and people could still be seen out in short sleeve shirts without jackets, so really we must've been looking late August the start of September, I can't remember which.

So, I said to Mel that I was going out for a few drinks with my friends, but was going to drive and not drink, and that wasn't a lie, I went and saw them at a pub before they went on into Birmingham for the rest of the night.

Me? I drove to the little Notebook house where the BMW was parked.

My delivery from eBay had been two magnetic signs for the sides of the car doors. They had only been £15 delivered for the both of them, and the advert showed it to be useful if you have your own little enterprise, like a dance school, or a magic show for kids parties, that kind of thing.

My enterprise was the successful no mess death of another person, and the long term evasion of the law, obviously I didn't put that on the magnetic signs.

No, the signs although not exactly the same as the original, claimed I was a taxi, working for 'Elite Cars' a genuine local taxi firm, it even included the genuine phone number for the taxi base and a little bit of artwork of a London style taxi.

It wasn't perfect but I didn't need it to be.

The signs were about 1ft by 1½ft, they were plastic coated on top of a flexible magnetic back, almost like a very large fridge magnet.

The signs simply sat on the outside of the two front doors, and with the size of the magnets, sat there quite comfortably without any danger of them slipping or coming free. After placing the first I stood back to make sure that it was level and see what it looked like from a bit of a distance.

It was convincing enough.

Now I've told you about this before, but bearing in mind it was so successful last time, I dug out my good little friend black electrical tape. I was of course going to alter the number plate again, it only made sense to try and keep the police away for as long as possible or at least make it more difficult.

So I got to work in altering the number plate, I turned the F into an E and the D into a B, again it wasn't perfect, but at a glance, and certainly from CCTV if they picked it up, it was enough to do the job.

Inside I placed a mobile phone holder onto the front windscreen, and a charger cable from the cigarette lighter, up towards the holder so I could put my mobile phone in there.

I also got myself a no smoking air freshener to hang from the rear view mirror, and another air freshener that said 'fasten your seatbelt' which I hung over the back of the front passenger seat so it could be seen from the rear seats. It meant I had to take the front passenger seat headrest out and hook the loop of the air freshener over the metal strut that holds into the back of the seat

before replacing the headrest.
It was all worth it though as these little things simply make the ruse that I am a genuine taxi all the more convincing.

It took me a while to sort this, but by the time I was ready to go out I was happy enough with what I had done and felt the taxi looked convincing enough to work to my advantage.

I put my bin liner and duct tape into the glovebox along with a couple of cable ties, I really didn't need anything else other than a victim.

Now I know it's a bit of a step away from home these days, but I decided that I'd go to my home town of Wolverhampton, where I was hoping I'd come across a victim easier than where I live now.

So back on the M5 and M6 for the half hour journey or so back to Wolverhampton, I started to get a slight feeling of butterflies in my tummy, not sure if it was excitement, nervousness or both.

FIFTY SIX

I landed in the town centre around quarter to midnight, which was about where I wanted it to be. It wasn't that late that there were going to be lots of fighting and lots of police knocking around, but late enough for there to be a few drunken folk.

Now I don't know why I hadn't thought of it before, but drunken people leave themselves so vulnerable that anything can and sometimes does happen to them.

As a drunk you are an ideal victim, you come across to the police as unreliable; you can't remember much of what has happened to you, you're sketchy, vague and unable to string a coherent sentence together and are completely unable to offer much in the way of a description about any potential offender.

OK, the only way my victim is going to talk to the police is via a séance, and I don't need to worry about these things; let's hope Whoopie Goldberg has retired.

So I drove down a road that says taxis only, and park up near to the man on the horse in the city centre, Yates's bar is opposite and there's a little parking bay, it's not designated for taxis but it's a great place for taxis to wait.

Whether it was luck or not that there were no other taxis there I'm not sure, but it was an ideal place with lots of drunken people walking around and not too much in the way of police.

There were a few police walking around on foot, but they weren't interested in me, they were going in and out of pubs and walking side by side just watching people mill around, I don't think I saw the same police officers twice.

I'd been parked up for a while, I'd had a couple of people come over to the car and ask if I was free, but they weren't drunk enough for what I wanted, so I said that I was waiting on a fare. Private hire cars aren't meant to pick people up who aren't booked, I mean they do, but they're not supposed to, so I had an excuse not to just let anyone in my car.

I needed to be patient, I had to get things right, I was risking a whole lot tonight and if it wasn't right I was behind bars in no time.

So I was nervous but happy to wait it out, then something horrific happened.

A scuffle broke on the opposite side of the road to Yates's about 100 yards in front of me, it wasn't a big scuffle, only about 6 people involved, with two main fighters and everyone else trying to split them up.

It was less than a minute and they were still pushing each other and I heard sirens, and in my rear view mirror saw a police car steaming up the road towards us.

Should I bail and get out of there, leave it for another night or risk waiting it? I couldn't decide.

My decision was made for me as a couple of police officers ran around the corner and split everyone up, one of the men fighting kept trying to have another swing at the other, despite the police being there, after the police car from behind pulled up, order had been restored.

The one guy who wouldn't stop trying to fight in spite of everything ended up on the floor at the hands of the police being handcuffed.

His opponent on the other hand had calmed down considerably, and was now swaying at the side of the road, acting very reasonably, there was a police officer talking to him, but I don't think much was sinking in.

I saw the officer reach into his pocket and pull out a piece of paper, he wrote something on it and handed it to the man swaying in the wind. The man stuffed it in his pocket without

171

looking at it.

As the police officer was about to leave the man also went to walk away, however he stumbled forward over himself, almost landing in a heap, but just about keeping on his feet; the officer quickly returned and steadied him.

The police officer started talking to the man, almost directly into his ear, but he didn't seem to be getting much back from him.

With one hand under his arm, the police officer walked the man over to my car, as they approached I saw he was about 25 years old, medium build and was really, really drunk.

I let the electric motor draw down the passenger window as the police officer approached, my heart was in my mouth, I couldn't believe what was going on, but I had no reason not to go along with it, what was the alternative? Screech away with my dodgy registration plate and magnetic taxi signs? No way, I had to be brave and see what happened.

I was scared though.

The police officer was very polite and asked me if I'd do him a favour and give the drunken man a lift home, I obviously agreed, and the officer opened my rear passenger door and helped the man into the back, he even leaned in and fastened his seatbelt.

I was glad of that little air freshener.

The police officer gave me an address in Bilston, which I inputted on my mobile phone attached to dash which was showing Google Maps.

I then set off with the police officers appreciation.

How funny, I was going to kill this man in the back of my car and the police showed their appreciation, you have to see the irony.

FIFTY SEVEN

Now, I don't know if this is the stuff you want to read about, or if you want to skip past it and prefer the mundane things about my life, but I'm going to kill him now, so read on or turn over its up to you.

The adrenaline must have been what kept him upright during the fight, because right now, as we drove through Heath Town, he was fast asleep.

At the lights past Heath Town I took a left and almost opposite the medical centre on the corner took another left, the road was completely deserted. On the one side was what I think was a deserted railway line, running below us, on the other, past the houses was an open field, and it was incredibly secluded for a drive only 5 minutes from the city centre.

I pulled over and put the hazard lights on; for a taxi, hazard lights give it the authority to park anywhere, it doesn't matter what the other road conditions are, hazard lights give a taxi impunity to all road laws.

I opened the glove box and took out what I needed.

I made sure the car was in neutral and turned the engine off, made sure the handbrake was on properly then got out and into the rear passenger seat next to him, he was still snoring.

The police officer had put him in the seatbelt which was perfect. During the journey and in his drunken state he had drooped into blissful slumber to one side, I suppose in a bid to try and lie down or become more comfortable, his head wasn't quite on middle seat of the rear bench seat because the seatbelt prevented it, but it was close. I reached through the space at his back and pulled his opposite arm into the small of his back, with his nearest arm I cable tied the two together, and as close to his back as I could.

173

He grumbled a little but didn't wake up.

I took the bin liner and tried opening it into a bag, I had to lick my fingers to get any purchase on the thing so that it would come apart even at the split. There wasn't enough room to open it by pulling it through the air, so I had to manually push out the bag, although I suppose it meant I didn't end up with a massive parachute, and was able to contain how far the bag opened.

I made sure the duct tape was nearby and the end of the tape was found an accessible.

I quickly put the bin liner over his head and made a grab for the duct tape; the bag over the head must have sparked his fight or flight response again and he instantly woke up. I grabbed hold of his shoulder with one hand to keep him in a prone position in the back seats, and luckily having prepared properly, started to tape the bag around his neck.

Even his drunken mind knew what was going on, and tried to resist, he was however restrained by a seatbelt, cable ties around his hands and he was helpless.

As the bag tightened around his neck and he struggled against the seatbelt and the cable ties, he started drawing in big gulps of breath, he was squirming and writhing on the back seat, trying to free his hands.

The cable ties dug into the skin on his wrists the more he moved and he was moaning really loud; I wouldn't say screaming but more like a low moan like he was trying to lift up weights or something, it was a sound that was guttural and came from deep within, it made me think he was doing everything within his power, making every effort to survive.

With all that squirming around and fuss, it took a lot of restraint not to either punch him the face or hit something off his head, he was a little irritating.

His writhing turned into a frenzy as the realisation that he was helpless became apparent, he started to kick out and used the back of the front seat and the passenger door as a fulcrum, but the seatbelt held him tight, before long the cable ties had dug into the skin of his writs and they were bleeding.

I imagine the car was shaking even from the outside as he struggled on the inside, I took a moment to evaluate my surroundings, and took a glance out of the windows to make sure there wasn't someone looking in on us, there was no-one around.

As the air was consumed in the bag, it became tight across his face, and he kind of created a vacuum, every time he tried to take a breath he was only able to draw in the plastic of the bag.

It really didn't take long for him to stop squirming, I'd say less than a minute, and before long I saw there was no attempt to draw any breath.

He was dead.

I sat back in the rear seat and exhaled hard, I think I'd been holding my breath while I was watching him die, pretty much like you do when you're watching a film and someone goes underwater, I don't know why but I hold my breath in line with them.

I took a moment to regain my composure, I mean I know I didn't do much, and the bag and ties did most of the work, but still, it was intense, my adrenaline had been pumping hard, my hands were shaking all the same.

I came to my senses and thought I needed to engage with the next part of the plan, before anyone stumbled across us in the car, sitting next to a corpse with a bag on its head is not what I want.

In any case, now the deed was done, I removed the bag, so he was just a sleeping passenger. The only problem was his eyes were wide open, and bulging; the white of his eyes were very veiny and red. He still looked like a corpse even without the bag,

175

but it was dark.

I went to get out of the car to carry on to the next stage in my plan, the child locks were on, I was stuck in the back.

FIFTY EIGHT

Having considered most things, why hadn't I considered the child locks? I cursed myself a little. This meant I had to clamber in-between the two front seats, it wasn't what I'd had in mind, but still it worked. I wasn't very agile, but managed to get myself back into the driver's seat.

I pulled away and headed towards Bilston, I wanted to get him a little bit closer to home.

After a short while, I realised he'd shit himself, it was starting to smell, I just hoped he didn't leave a stain on the seats.

Not too far from the town centre of Bilston there a small side road that leads to a kind of estuary, which is just before/after a series of locks on the canal. It's a good access point to the canal system and there is a small car park.

I was expecting to see perhaps a car parked in there with a couple of young lovers, but no it was empty, and I was able to pull straight in.

I made sure the rear passenger side door was water's side and as close to the canal as possible, there were bollards that prevented cars getting too close, but I thought it wasn't too far to drag him.

I reached into the glovebox, I'd remembered to tuck a small pair of pliers in there; I'd need them for the cable ties.

I got out of the car and went around to his side and opened the door, the smell of shit hit me first, it was quite bad, I had to reach inside and unclip his seatbelt, the dirty bastard was making me gag.

I kept the cable ties on his wrists, I didn't want to remove them until the last moment, his arms would make a great anchor point for dragging and he was going to be a dead weight, get it? Dead weight, he was dead....never mind.

I hauled him out of the back of the car and he landed hard on the floor, he was lighter than I expected, but it till took some effort to drag him across the small amount of canal bank.

Once he was on the edge, I used the pliers to clip the cable ties, and kicked him the rest of the way into the water. He bobbed on the top, face down, it looked really odd.

I walked back to the car and opened the boot, I put the cable tie and the magnetic signs in there, I then unpicked the tape from the registration and crumpled it all together in my fingers, I put that in the boot too.

I took the pliers, and the tape from the back seat and put these in the glove box, the death bag, I put that in the boot with the other perishable stuff that needed to be disposed of.

I got back into the car, started it up and pulled out of the car park, once far enough away from him, I settled back into my chair and tried to relax. I needed a cup of tea, I knew that much, but in all honestly I was pleased. Things had run incredibly smoothly, I couldn't have expected better really, so a big pat on the back for me.

Unlike the others, this one had been so easy too, I had barely put any effort in, the ties, belt and of course the bag had done all the work, I'd just sat back and let it all happen; I couldn't think there'd be much to roll over in my mind about this one. Nothing to really claw at me or cause that niggle in my mind, and those pesky egg cracking thoughts hopefully all but dispelled.

I turned on the radio The Eagles were singing about how there's going to be a heartache tonight, I chuckled to myself. How apt.

FIFTY NINE

I took the drive back towards home at a leisurely pace, bearing in mind how much I'd paid for this BMW, it had performed admirably. I was very pleased with it, and who knows, it could come in useful again.

I parked it up in the long driveway, which was almost a road in itself that led to The Notebook house, and collected my everyday car that I'd parked up.

I checked the clock on the way back to my little cottage where Mel would be sleeping, it was just after 1am, which was still quite reasonable for having been out with my friends.

After pulling up outside I steadied myself before going inside, it was in darkness and I didn't want to disturb Mel if I could help it, so I was careful when unlocking, opening and closing the front door. I tiptoed into the kitchen and closed the door to the hallway.

It was done and I was safe back home, the first thing I did was put the kettle on. I knew I would need to come to terms with what I had done, and it wasn't an easy thing to put everything straight in my mind, but the extended journey had partway done the job. There were great swathes of the trip along the motorway that I couldn't remember, and I suppose this was my mind trying to repair itself after the grisly game of murder.

I sat on the sofa with a fresh cup of tea, and felt engulfed by the comfort, I hadn't exerted as much as I had in the past, but it still took its toll, I could've fell straight off to sleep.

There was a kiss on my forehead, and all of a sudden Mel was standing there.

She had heard me come in and when I hadn't come upstairs after a while she had come down to find me dozed off on the sofa, a full cup of tea in my hand. She had taken the tea from me and

179

awoken me in the best possible way.

She took me by the hand and led me upstairs, I said I would need a shower before bed, I didn't want these death hands and clothes coming anywhere near my beautiful Mel.

I stripped off and took a shower, which was so revitalising, it made me feel great, it was almost a symbolic way of washing the horrid deeds of the day off my skin and down the drain.

With my mind in order and my skin now clean, I felt ready to finally get into bed beside Mel. I put my clothes in the wash basket in the bathroom, and decided that I would wash them separately from anything else for the first wash since his death.

My hair was still a little damp, it was short so it didn't take a lot of drying, and I gave it an extra rough rub with a towel. I then sat on the toilet for a few moments, seat down, to both let my hair dry a little and finally adjust myself before being with Mel.

When I got into the bedroom, Mel was already asleep again, I looked at her lying there for a while, enjoying the sight. She looked so peaceful and beautiful and my heart filled with love for her, she was so gentle and kind, and now carrying our child, I felt truly blessed. She didn't know I was looking, but it was another one of my lovely little moments shared with her.

She had left my space next to her with the duvet pulled back over her creating a little triangle of space for me to easily climb into. I got in and pulled my side of the duvet from her and covered myself, she gave a slight sigh as the covers moved and my weight adjusted the mattress.

As I lay back and rested my head on the pillow, I closed my eyes then realised I needed to set an alarm, I wanted to be up fairly early, there was something I needed to do. Alarm set I lay back and gently drifted off to sleep.

SIXTY

Breakfast in bed.

I got up early, Mel stirred as I got out of bed, but I don't think she woke up. I grabbed my dressing gown and went downstairs.

I went to the freezer and picked out a pack of sausages we had bought fresh but frozen and pinged them into the microwave to defrost. I took the eggs out and placed them on the counter.

Ok, sausage and egg sandwich wasn't as nice as a full breakfast, but better than bran flakes.

Once the sausages were well on the way, I took out another pan, I took the first egg and split it with a knife...

Nothing, no gory flashback, just me breaking an egg.

It seemed last night had worked the trick, I had cured myself. With the baby coming along and how I now wanted to be, that was important, I was quietly pleased with myself and my triumph.

Breakfast in bed very rarely works, unless there is a concerted effort by the sleeper to remain in bed, the sizzling the smells and the clunking of cutlery generally brings someone downstairs. As was the way with Mel this morning.

She sat at the table in the 'dining room' part of the open plan kitchen, and when the sandwich was delivered she ate it hungrily.

We spent the rest of Sunday in our dressing gowns meandering around the house, I spent some time on the PS4 and Mel was catching up on some reading. It was really pleasant and relaxing, well I say relaxing, but getting shot at almost every corner on Call of Duty, probably by a 13 year old boy started to get frustrating quite quickly.

The day rushed by really, and before I knew it we were cuddled up on the sofa in the dark watching a film before bed.

I hadn't seen the news and had put the dead drunk to the back of my mind, a day like today had been just what I needed just to build that extra barrier for myself, so that I could function normally.

Sleep came easy, whether that's unique for someone who has done what I've done, I might never know, but the old phrase about being kept up at night didn't apply. I felt that I'd overcame what I'd done already and was ready for the week ahead, I honestly felt at peace. No doubt you hate that thought.

We both got up at pretty much the same time the next morning, with Mel having further to go, she always left before me and was generally home after me, before she left for work, she reminded me of the Dr's appointment for this evening to get the ball rolling regarding the baby. As if I'd need reminding of that.

I put the TV on before I left for work, no discovery of a murdered body, the news was full of loads of other shit but nothing to do with me. I high fived myself on the way out to the car.

The drive to work was fairly easy, I'd fallen into enjoying Heart FM on the way in, it was local and the guys in the morning were funny, also, I was quickly approaching that age where the music on other stations had started to sound like noise.

The news however, being local, did mention police investigating a body in a Bilston canal, I was kind of expecting it so it wasn't a surprise. The surprise came later.

SIXTY ONE

What a complete waste of time. It was so condescending and it felt like I was a child at school again, maybe they did have to deal with brain dead halfwits most of the time, but to tarnish everyone with the same brush is so demoralising.

At the Dr's appointment they asked Mel some questions about why she thought she might be pregnant and then questions about her period to try and gauge the probable number of weeks she was pregnant, Mel then had to provide a sample, which was checked with pretty much the same kind of pregnancy test we'd already used three of.

When the Dr declared she was pregnant, it was completely stating the obvious and I was unimpressed.

The only positive thing from the appointment was to have a midwife assigned and to get ourselves in line for a proper ultrasound scan.

As we left, Mel was asking me to behave as I was chuntering about the entire appointment, she was laughing too at my sarcastic rantings. I was very tongue in cheek with my criticism of the process which made Mel laugh.

On the way home is when the surprise came, obviously Heart FM was still on the radio as we had taken my car.

The news came on, and although the big story was some kind of rubbish going on in very important London, which really had no effect on people outside of London at all, the following story was about a murder investigation of a reveller on Saturday night.

Murder? Already? Jesus, I thought it would take at least the coroner to decide it was murder over misadventure.

It was barely two days and they were already looking at murder, prior to the post mortem. This wasn't what I had anticipated, I mean I expected a few days even a week or more before they came to that conclusion.

Don't worry, it didn't spark anything off in me, I'm not going back out killing. Yet.

I considered what the police had to go on.

A make and model of a car, but an erroneous number plate, with no clear images of the driver. They weren't going to find the car, not a chance, even if they worked out the right registration and managed to follow it up the motorway; they would never find where it had been parked.

Now him, I'd barely touched him, and the materials used to kill him were safe in the boot of the never to be found car.

In my opinion they had even less to go on with this guy than any of the others, and that is what I mean when I said I didn't like gore and moved away from this as my murders went on. This one was pretty goreless, if that's even a word.

The lack of exertion, and any real evidence, gave me a confident kind of feeling that this was going nowhere, so I was unconcerned realistically that it was already a murder investigation.

I chuckled to myself at the thought of the frustrations the police must be feeling right about now.

In all honesty I wasn't even sure they'd be able to link it to the others, I think most of the evidence was in the car and without that, it would just be a standalone murder.

As I could have expected really, with the culmination of the stress and intensity of what I did on the Saturday, linked with the excitement of getting everything confirmed regarding the baby, during the journey home I started to develop a bit of a headache.

By the time I reached home it was crippling and it felt like someone was stabbing a screwdriver through my eye. I didn't want to make a big deal out of it, sometimes I had migraines like these, I just said to Mel that I had a bit of a headache and took some Ibuprofen.

After about half an hour the pain had subsided, and I was able to engage with Mel better about baby names.

We were still talking about whether we'd find out the sex when the time came and the pros and cons for finding out. We each had a list of names that we liked that we could start to whittle down.

It was enjoyable talking about it, it gave me hope. I would free myself of these murders and wipe the slate clean, Saturday's was the last, and from now on I had a separate purpose.

If I hadn't been caught for the others already, I had clearly got away with them, and there were no significant leads. Like I say, this last one, they had absolutely nothing to go on and I was confident that I wouldn't be brought to justice for it.

So that would be it, no more murder, concentrate on being a dad, and put everything else to the back of my mind.

Good intentions are so hard to keep.

SIXTY TWO

Where does life go? I don't mean me, draining it away from someone, I was thinking more about the time, and how quick life flashes past.

Over the last few weeks I'd made some tentative digging around the old Notebook house, checking things on the internet with a view of trying to find an owner and how to go about contacting someone for a price for it.

I'd also been unable to stop shopping, I'd bought a few bodysuits and bibs in yellows, browns and greens, asexual colours that could be used no matter the sex, I found that this had really occupied my mind.

We'd also been looking at travel systems, I thought they were pushchairs and car seat, but no, we were looking at travel systems. Don't get me wrong they're impressive things, well thought out, light and easy to store, but my goodness expensive; I'd got a whole BMW to kill someone in for the same price.

Anyway, I wanted our little one to be as safe as possible, both of our cars were fitted with Isofix, which I'd never heard of before, so it made sense to go for this style, it was safer and easier to use.

Before we knew it really the first 12 week scan was on us, and we were at the hospital awaiting our turn to be called in to the unit. It was very exciting, this was going to be the first time we would actually see our child.

When our turn came we held hands into the small room, and the radiologist introduced herself and said what was going to happen, Mel lay on the couch and lifted her t-shirt exposing her tummy. The nurse turned on the monitors and squirted gel over Mel's tummy then started to use the equipment to find our child.

She had found it, I turned my head from side to side and

couldn't see what she was talking about, it was a series of dark and lighter undefined shapes that I couldn't see any kind of familiarity to.

The she pointed out, it looked a little bit like a peanut, a peanut with a heartbeat.

I was beside myself, how great, I could only imagine how Mel felt, it was incredible, and I loved that little peanut from that moment.

The nurse took some measurements and screenshots, so that we could take a picture home with us, we had more of an exact age too, due to the measurements somehow. What a fantastic feeling though, there was our little child, slowly growing and forming, a little life safely nestled in my Mel.

It's hard to describe my emotions, becoming a dad is simply one of the most amazing, wonderful feelings that I have ever experienced, and seeing it for the first time, seeing that wonderful little child, I had a little bit of a cry, I don't mind saying.

As soon as we came out of the cubicle, I gave Mel a big hug and a kiss, we had to wait a few minutes for the scan picture, but it was worth the wait. Now it was easier to see the little head forming and the arched back. Wow.

We decided to head to my parents' house as they were closest and pass on the good news, I couldn't wait to see their faces.

When we went in to see them I said that I wanted them to have a look at a photo, I'd taken a picture of the scan onto my phone and showed them the scan.

They couldn't work out what it was at first then they looked at me, eyes wide, and I told them they were going to be grandparents, I have to say that was another wonderful feeling. They were overjoyed.

We stayed with them into the evening and shared a Chinese takeaway together, as Mel's parents were living quite a bit further away, we decided we would go up and see them over the weekend coming up.

I could tell Mel felt the love from my parents as I did, they were genuinely over the moon for us.

I have to say that this is a genuinely happy time that is filled with love.

By the time the weekend came and we were with Mel's parents giving them the news, our house had been scattered with loads of cards and little presents from my side of the family.

Mel's parents were absolutely identical, they had been grandparents before, as Mel was the youngest child, but they were still ecstatic with the news.

In the same way as Mel felt it from my parents, I felt it from hers, they loved me.

I know you hate the idea of people loving me, but they don't know. It's only us that know, and you only retrospectively, to them, I was the best thing that had happened to Mel; we loved each other and were happy, and that is what any parent wants for their child.

Now, the next part of my life is a bit of a blur, a lot happens in a short space of time, I'll try and be as open as I can and tell you as much as possible, just to let you know I'm sure there's loads I miss

It's probably a good three weeks before anything else raises hits head. Raises its head it does though.

SIXTY THREE

Mel shouted my name.

I wasn't quite awake, and like my scream ages ago now, I wasn't exactly sure I heard it, or whether it was part of some dream or something. Mel wasn't lying next to me.

Mel shouted my name again, she seemed urgent.

It was kind of like an autonomic response, my agility in getting out of bed, and finding myself wide awake to the sound of her voice.

As I walked into the bathroom, my hands were shaking a little, the tone she had used to call my name had set me on edge a little; it was an odd feeling to have.

Mel was on the toilet and was looking tearful, I looked around for a broken mirror or bottle of expensive perfume or something. Eventually I turned to her and held my arms out and asked her what was up.

She didn't say anything, but held out her arms for me to go over and hug her.

I called her sweetheart and asked her what was up, had she had some bad news somewhere, I was holding her as I was asking her.

She pulled away and looked at me in my face, her eyes connected to mine and she solemnly shook her head, then collapsed in on herself in a kind of sitting scrunch her head almost on her knees.

She started to weep, and started to apologise to me.

I couldn't understand what was going on, something was most certainly wrong, but I couldn't work it out. My Mel needed me

189

and I bent down and hugged her curled up frame, I lay gentle kisses on the back of her neck.

I asked her again what was wrong, and through the weeping she started to say something, but I couldn't make it out. Her weep developed into a long drawn out shriek. The sound of which I have never heard her make before, it was pain, but she was uninjured.

I started to stroke her exposed back, in a bid to try and comfort her somehow, I didn't know what had made her so upset, but I'd never seen her like this and I was starting to get worried.

I tried again asking her what was wrong, she was unable to answer through her tears, instead she crumpled further, sliding off the toilet to the right hand side, I supported her weight as she collapsed and she lay in a ball to the side of the toilet, my arms still holding onto her.

This was by far the most bizarre start to a day I think I'd ever had.

It was the smear of blood on the toilet seat that made me stand up, my caresses for Mel giving way to my dread.

I stood and looked into the bowl.

It was filled with blood, fresh blood like she was actively bleeding from a deep cut, and large clumps of clotted blood, my heart was an my mouth, I knew what this meant.

I stood there, transfixed. Mel was sobbing on the floor, curled into a ball and I was looking at the blood.

I felt my own blood drain from me, and I went light headed, almost to the point of passing out.

No, No, It can't be true. No, this can't be happening. No, there's no way this is real. Please someone, wake me up, please this can't be right. Please, I beg of you, say I'm dreaming; say this isn't really what I'm seeing. Say everything is going to be ok.

It couldn't have been long, but it felt an eternity, standing there looking at the blood. Looking at my little baby, nothing more than clots of blood floating in the toilet.

I screamed. A proper scream, loud and full with all of my lungs.

My heart broke, and it was the greatest feeling of loss I'd ever experienced, my baby was gone, my little child, my beautiful little child was gone.

I wanted to thrust my hands into that blood, draw it out and hug it close to me. Smear myself with it, I wanted to show it the love I felt for it, and the loss I was feeling overcame me.

I dropped onto my knees, in much the same way that Mel had collapsed in on herself.

I'd lost all awareness of her crying on the floor, so encumbered with my own emotions I was, I wanted to hold her, but I wanted someone to hold me too.

I didn't know what to do, I honestly wanted to scoop everything out of the toilet and hold it, like it was a tiny baby in my arms. I wanted that blood to represent everything that I had ever wanted and everything I had ever dreamed of, I wanted that blood to know and feel that I loved it with all of my heart.

Involuntarily my hands were clutching the sides of my head, they had a firm grip on the hair at the sides, almost looping my ears.

I couldn't bear it, call it irrational, but I ran out of the bathroom and to the small bedroom that was designated as a nursery, I emptied two, three, four carrier bags of presents onto the floor, until I found a large comfy blanket. I'd remembered buying it a while ago, it had the emblem of a little teddy bear on one corner. It was light brown almost chenille type fabric, with dark brown edges. It was soft and luxurious.

191

I ran back into the bathroom with it, Mel was still lying in exactly the same place crying.

I did exactly what I considered was the right thing to do, given the circumstances. I couldn't bear the thought that my baby, my little child was going to be just flushed away, there's no way I was going to let that happen.

I lay the blanket out, and using my hands scooped out the clotted blood, it ran from the gaps in my fingers, but I didn't care, I scooped back into the toilet for more, and again and again, until I was unable to retrieve anything further from the bowl.

The blanket did not look appealing. It was a blood soaked rag, but if ever anyone had said such a thing about it I would've stood up and gouged their eyes out. This blanket was my baby.

I folded the blanket so that the contents were hidden, but the way I folded it, I wanted it to be a swaddled baby, one corner in at the bottom, then both sides, one over the other.

I picked up the blanket, and held it close to my chest like I was cradling a baby, the tears were streaming down my face and I was crying uncontrollably.

I'm not saying that Mel was insignificant, but my own grief and loss overwhelmed me, more perhaps than my feelings of love.

I dropped onto my back, clutching the blanket, crying and shouting the lone word 'No'. Like this would somehow change things, like this would turn back time and prevent this from happening. Like me begging, pleading and not accepting it, would change things. It wouldn't.

Mel didn't need a Dr to know, she was a mum; she already knew that it was over.

In a brief moment of clarity I had dialled 999, and the ambulance crew that turned up were empathic, they showed so much respect and understanding, I kind of got the impression this was not the first time they had borne witness to such a scenario.

To be fair to them, they didn't try and take the blanket from me, and after a while Mel had joined me in clinging onto it. We held onto each other, and held onto the blanket it like we were a family.

SIXTY FOUR

For some reason Mel was apologising to me, as we sat together, holding onto the blanket that contained our baby.

Why she would think that I could possibly blame her I didn't know. This was an absolute travesty, no doubt about that at all, but I didn't blame Mel, not in the slightest.

I left Mel with the blanket and went to strip the bed, there was a small patch of blood there. I would have to throw the bottom sheet away, I wouldn't be able to sleep on it again; as the sheet came off the bed and I scrunched it up I gave it a kiss before going out to the bin. It was symbolic for me and I needed to do it. I didn't want Mel having to do it.

Although I was heartbroken I wanted to try and stay as strong as I could. I wanted to be there for Mel, who I'm sure still had a lot of horrible times to come.

The ambulance crew said that all of her vitals, blood pressure, heart rate etc. were fine and that she didn't have to go with them if she didn't want to. They gave us the obvious bad news that there was no heart beat any longer, and that we would have to be checked out by a midwife and probable ultrasound, to see if there was anything left inside.

They said to expect more blood, oh I was sure there was going to be more blood.

I know what you're thinking, this is a spark again for me, that I'm about to go on a rampage. We'll talk about that later.

I also suppose you think this is a little strike of karma. I've taken loved ones from others, I've ended someone's life prematurely and left those who loved them empty, heartbroken and lost.

Now it's my turn.

194

To feel love for someone who I'll never get to hold, to feel their absence and the emptiness that I will never be in their company. For me to be forever thinking about what could've been, what life would have been like, to miss what I never had for the rest of my days.

Well shame on you. You are talking about being happy that my child died. My child was innocent, and nothing deserved to happen to it. I have done some bad things, but my child hadn't, that's just being spiteful.

So I'm sure you're pleased to know that I am consumed with grief, the reason is not what you would have wanted, but you're happy all the same that I feel this way, I deserve to feel what I have made others endure.

That doesn't change the fact that I am loved, that I feel love and will steel myself to get through this, I will be a rock for Mel and whatever it takes, we will get through this together.

Your bitterness aside, my inner strength is indomitable, I have shown throughout what I have told you that I have an ability to cope, to survive and endure. I will make sure that this is the same, my grief shall always be with me, but I will function, I will continue.

I returned to Mel, who was still taking comfort from the blanket, but had moved back to our bed, the bed had no covers but it was still comfortable and the best place to be for now.

I cuddled up to her and she sobbed.

I let her cry uncontrollably, making no comment, offering no comfort other than my embrace until she reached a point that she could cry no more. She looked at me in my eyes, and with the deepest heartfelt look, she apologised again.
I did my best to reassure her, I told her how she was not to blame, and how much I loved her. I held her tight, and gently kissed her head.

I will never forget the look of broken failure she gave me, without a word it said, I failed you and our baby; I wasn't a good enough mum.

Words can't do my feelings justice, either about how I feel at the loss, or how to describe to Mel that she is not a failure, to either me or our baby. It's a shame you can't somehow give someone your feelings, so that they understand, the words used to describe them are inadequate.

SIXTY FIVE

Remember, right at the beginning, I said I'd never had any kids, well, I wasn't lying.

It's like that simple word Necessity though, there's a story that comes with that simple sentence. I'm not sure whether it was something you'd considered at the outset or not, but there it is. I never become a dad.

My workplace gave me two weeks compassionate leave when they found out what had happened. It's weird, they would've only given me two weeks paternity leave if everything had worked out, and I would've needed more than that I'm sure.

Anyway, we ended up with an emergency appointment two days afterwards, once the midwife unit were aware.

The results showed that there was no remaining foetus, and that there was nothing more that was needed to be done, nature had taken its course and no further intervention from them was required. They were apologetic but, it was business as normal for them.

We left downhearted and tried to find solace in a couple of drinks and a pub meal.

We didn't really speak much and clearly Mel felt responsible, and no matter what I said, she didn't seem to take it on board. I mean, she listened to me, and agreed every now and then, but she was distant, I could tell that she wasn't really agreeing with me, but just didn't want an argument.

When we got home, she had another glass of wine and went to bed, I sat on my own downstairs, the TV on, but not really watching it.

When I went up to bed, Mel was fast asleep, she was huddled in a ball holding herself, and when I got into bed she didn't move, or make a noise. I wasn't sure she was actually asleep, if she was she didn't say anything. I wanted to hug her, but wasn't sure she wanted that with her position; I didn't want to wake her if she was asleep, but I wanted to comfort her, it was hard to know what to do, I lay on my back and fell asleep.

Little things make all the difference, and I can see that now looking back, right then though, I didn't know; like I've said before, hindsight is a wonderful thing.

Mel hadn't been asleep and she wanted nothing more than for me to hold her, I know that now, but I couldn't have known back then.

Now, there was something that we had to discuss, and the next day, we talked about what we were going to do with the blanket. We agreed we wanted to bury it, properly like a funeral, and we wanted a headstone.

I didn't give a fuck if other people who had had a miscarriage had done anything similar, this was our lives and it's what we wanted.

We called the blanket Jamie Millie, it was both a girl and a boy name and we organised a deed of grant for the cemetery.

You may call us weird, or stupid, but it was our way of grieving and letting go.

With all the things we needed to sort and get ready, the two weeks flew by, before I knew it, it was Sunday night and I was preparing for work the next day.

Mel hadn't changed in mood, she was heartbroken, and I didn't want to go back but there was no choice.

SIXTY SIX

When I went back to work, there was a condolences card for me, and they had paid for a large bunch of flowers for Mel. It was very kind and I thanked them for being so kind.

The first day was readjusting and catching up on developments since I'd been away, there was a couple of backlogged things that I needed to sort out, but mainly it was emails and a couple of meetings.

The first day didn't really drag, and I hadn't allowed any thoughts of murder creep into my mind, I had occupied myself pretty much most of the day and the time had flown by. I'd been in contact with Mel via text throughout the day who hadn't returned to work yet, rightly so too.

When I got home, and walked in the house, I couldn't find Mel to start with, I left the flowers downstairs on the kitchen table and went upstairs and found her in bed, pretty much where I'd left her.

There was a breakfast bowl to the side of the bed, and when I walked in Mel turned over and greeted me with a smile, she held her arms out for me to go over to hug her. I did so gladly.

As soon as her head landed on my shoulder she started sobbing, I could tell by her eyes, that she had been that way for some time.

Don't get me wrong, I was upset, I'd seen a man walking down the street holding his daughters hand on the way home, and it had made me cry; I bet he didn't even realise how lucky he was, he was so accustomed to her being there.

I had managed to control myself enough though, that meant I was able to function and continue with things, and I could see Mel was struggling to come to terms with it fully. Perhaps I just have that mental fortitude that some people don't have. Let's face it, I've faced and done a lot of horrendous things in my life and got past them.

I stayed that way with Mel for what seemed like ages, I whispered that I should make us dinner and she grumbled, and said we should just get a takeaway, I wasn't opposed to that; so I ordered Indian food for delivery.

I went downstairs and put the flowers in a vase, I then took them up to our bedroom, where Mel had stayed and explained where they were from. I put them on the chest of drawers and went back downstairs, I tidied up the kitchen a little and sent the vacuum cleaner around the downstairs.

When the doorbell rang, I collected the food and paid the driver, I had set out two plates on the kitchen counter. I divvied up the food between us and poured a glass of wine for Mel, I shouted up that dinner was ready and Mel asked if she could have hers upstairs.

I took hers up to her, but I couldn't eat on the bed, so I went downstairs and caught up with the news.

Obviously it was national news so nothing cropped up about my murder, I remembered the report on Heart FM had given me his name, but I'd been driving and couldn't remember it. Something was ringing at the back of my mind that it was an old fashioned name like Colin or something.

Anyway, I had to leave some of my food, as there was a lot. I had had a cup of tea with mine, and after the last little sip I went upstairs to see how Mel was getting on; the food had barely been touched if anything had at all, but the glass had been drained.

I asked if she was ok and Mel gave me a bit of a scowl that said, of course not. Idiot. She asked for a refill of her glass, and to take her food away, she'd got no appetite. I duly obliged with what she wanted.

I put her leftovers in a plastic tub and put it in the fridge, which would do for me at work the next day.

I refilled her glass and took it up to her, she sat up in the bed and asked me about my day, cradling the glass and taking long sips. I said that not much had happened and that I was just getting through my emails.

By the time I was done talking about work, and to be honest, that didn't take me very long, she had sunk her second glass of wine and held it out to me in a gesture that said 'more please'.

I went back downstairs and refilled the glass, I made self a cup of tea while I was on it. I returned to Mel, with a drink for both of us, and sat down with her. She took the glass, but I gestured for her to put it on the bedside cabinet. I got in close and gave her long hug.

I didn't say anything, I just held her.

As soon as we parted she picked up the glass and started drinking with those long sips. I asked her how she had been, but she just shrugged her shoulders.

This wasn't like Mel at all, I hadn't seen her drink like this, or spend a day in bed. I mean she had been down with the flu one week, and even then she was out of the bed doing stuff. This wasn't like her at all, and I was a little bit worried about her.

I didn't know what to say, I didn't know whether I should say I was worried, or give her some more time; I knew her drinking wasn't the answer she was after, but in the short term, it wasn't going to harm her more than the hangover, so I decided to let it be for now.

I promised myself, that if it continued I'd intervene. It didn't continue, but I'll tell you about that in a while.

SIXTY SEVEN

I'd probably got the first week of being back at work under my belt, when I was struck with the thoughts of having to kill someone.

Whether it was a delayed reaction, or what, I don't know, but it hit me that after everything that had happened recently, I was more than ever justified in taking a life of my own.

If there was ever a reason, this was it; I didn't need that niggle, or to try and escape thoughts of previous events, no, this was revenge almost. I felt entirely justified in killing someone else.

With that in mind I set about a plan, without having to be constrained by being a good father and role model any longer, I was free to act with impunity. With impunity I would act.

Now I'd been thinking about things like this in the past, and during the planning for other murders I'd thought about this, but had ended up going with different plans.

It seemed really easy, and I considered that it would be pretty easy to get away with, so I suppose, in the void of anything better; I returned to past plans.

So, really apart from Emma, who was the start of all this mess, I'd always taken on people who were effectively in a vulnerable position. Alone in the woods, working illicitly with very few safeguards, or as in the last one, completely smashed on booze.

Who better then to target for my next murder? Exactly, the vulnerable.

Kids? Are you having a laugh, you wouldn't say that to my face; no, never that would never happen. I know what I've done, but I would protect a child, look after it if it was lost, there is absolutely no way I could ever think of harming a child. I'm bad, but I'm not that bad, that is an underlined in bold with capitals and a larger font **NO NO** for me.

I don't think I want to go into too much detail now, because it's something to keep you interested in what I have to say, and we still have a little way to go yet; but my next target is someone vulnerable. I figure that I'll need that trusty old BMW.

Anyway, it's the end of the first week back at work. Mel is due back next week, but I can't see that happening to be honest, she's barely out of bed, and I've taken up all the slack at home in terms of the housework and cooking. Which I honestly don't mind, I want Mel to take her time and get past things, she'll move on, I know she will, and as long as I support her and look after her, it's just a matter of time.

On my way home, I start to develop my migraine again, it only starts off slight, as a dull ache behind my eyes, but before long it progresses into a stabbing pain behind one of my eyes. I usually have a good hour before it gets to the stage where I'm in real pain.

I'm close enough to home to know that I'll be back before it gets too bad and I can treat myself with some tablets and a cup of tea.

As I pulled into the driveway it was reaching the point where I almost had to close one of my eyes to keep the pain slightly at bay. I don't know why it helped, but I put my hand over my closed eye, like an eye patch, it should have no medicinal purpose but it seemed to help.

Once in the house I helped myself to a cup of tea and my ibuprofen, Mel was upstairs again, and it was clear to see that she hadn't been up.

I went upstairs and peeked in on Mel, she was fast asleep in the bed, I saw that there was an empty glass with the remnants of the red wine in the bottom next to the bed.

I went back downstairs and picked up my cup of tea, and collapsed onto the sofa letting the painkillers attack the pain with the help of hot tea, I decided that I would give Mel a few more days, then I would have to say something.

I dozed off on the sofa, but with the weekend on us, I thought that it didn't matter if I did allow myself to doze off. I certainly had no plans, at least I wouldn't be able to kill anyone yet; I hadn't got all the plans in place.

Let's face it, I have a lot on my plate at the moment, getting everything sorted about killing someone was towards the back of the list. Taking care of Mel was right at the forefront.

SIXTY EIGHT

When I awoke it had only just gone 7pm, so there was still plenty of the evening left. My headache had gone to my relief, and I thought I might try and tempt Mel out of bed.

I went upstairs with my mobile phone and sat on the end of the bed, Mel stirred and gave me a smile. That was more like my Mel. She stretched out her arms and gave a yawn.

I asked if she was ok, which wasn't really answered, and she asked me how my day had been. Not much had happened, I work in an office, but I said I'd had another migraine, and she suggested I check it out at the Dr the following week. I promised I would.

Anyway, I went on to say that there was a decent film out and that she we should go out and have a look.

I didn't know what to expect, whether she would be up for it or not.

When she got out of bed and headed towards the bathroom I was over the moon, it looked like I wouldn't have to say anything after all. I shouted through the bathroom door, that a large bag of sweet popcorn and cup of coke were on the cards too.

When I went downstairs, I almost skipped into the kitchen.

I know we had shared a tragedy, but we still had to carry on and live our lives, and I was pleased to see that Mel was finally getting better, and coming to terms with things.

I tidied up my cup and decided to slip myself a couple more ibuprofen as I didn't want anything to interrupt this evening, I generally tidied, but there wasn't much to clean as Mel had been upstairs most of the day it seemed.

I went upstairs and collected the glass next to the bed, as I'd done most of the tidying I placed this in the sink, I treated myself to a chocolate bar, then when I went to put wrapper in the bin, found the three bottles of emptied wine.

It was a bit of a shock, but I suppose it was over now as Mel was finally up and out of bed, and I had coaxed her into having a good time.

Back in the bedroom I splashed myself with some aftershave and changed my clothes, I didn't really need a shower, and could always have one when I got back. I made the bed, but then lay back on the pillows resting my eyes while Mel showered.

I closed my eyes and started to relax, I took a deep breath, and let the air fill my lungs. With my eyes closed, it allowed my ears to take up more of my senses and I could hear the shower running in the bathroom.

I concentrated on the shower, and it was regular and uninterrupted, there were no splashes, the kind of splashes of water you'd expect to hear when washing your hair, or washing away the shower gel.

Instead I could hear convulsing and coughing. I realised that Mel was being sick.

How could I have been so silly, Mel had been up in bed for a few days now, and had gone through quite a bit of wine, how could I possibly think that she would be ok to just get up and go out with no issues. I was surprised her sickness had arrived so soon in fact.

It's crazy when you think about it, I mean I'm a grown up and have had my fair share of hangovers and the aftermath of heavy drinking.

I couldn't have seen it at the time, but now I was seeing the results of getting up, I couldn't believe I'd be so stupid. The door to the bathroom was closed, I gave the door a knock before trying the handle, it was locked. I put my head against the door and listened into the room, Mel was still coughing and I could hear her retching.

It was a sound I knew all too well, she had been sick and emptied her stomach. There couldn't have been much there to throw up to be honest as she had barely eaten, so I could tell that she was now retching on an empty stomach. Convulsing hard, but nothing coming out, it was one of the most horrible feelings being sick.

I tried to talk to Mel through the door, but I think she was a little pre-occupied. I went downstairs and got a glass of water, and the last two ibuprofen tablets.

My thoughts of going out and watching a film of a sudden replaced by the thought of a long night ahead caring for a very hungover Mel.

At least hopefully it would be the last of the drinking.

SIXTY NINE

Just as I thought, it was a long night. Despite Mel wanting wine over water, I refused and she was in no fit state to argue otherwise.

It was odd, she pleaded for the wine, like it was medicine, as if the wine might somehow cure her; it would have perhaps taken away the hangover in a hair of the dog kind of way, but that just prolonged the pain to be honest, and it was better to start the process now.

She was clearly suffering with a terrible headache, she was pawing at her hair, trying to rub her head better. I knew that feeling too, especially with my recent run of migraines.

The ibuprofen had clearly had little effect, but to be fair, with what she had drank over the past few days, she was going to be due a massive headache and hangover.

I bought in a large bath towel from the bathroom, and lay it next to her. There was nothing for her to bring up, but the convulsions continued. I think the most she bought up was the water that she used to take the ibuprofen; the towel was there to protect the pillows, and she convulsed over it, but in all honesty he pillows were safe as nothing was coming out.

By 2am Mel had gone back to sleep and I chanced some sleep myself.

I went out like a light, despite my earlier snooze. I had been a little bit frightened about going to sleep, for what I might wake up to, but sleep came quickly.

When I awoke there was no Mel lying next to me and I checked my watch, I'd slept straight through to 9am. As I passed the bathroom there was the smell of shower gel and shampoo and it looked like Mel had had a shower.

Downstairs I found Mel on the sofa in the living room, she was cradling a cup of tea and the news was on the TV.

I asked how she was feeling and then went on to have a full conversation with her; as we were talking I was thinking about how great it was to have some of my Mel back. She got up and hugged me, and my heart melted all over again.

This was the best I'd felt in a long time, and certainly since what had happened to us.

Mel nibbled at a slice of toast that I made her, her appetite was clearly still far step away from an Indian takeaway, but slowly she was recovering, and that pleased me.

With Mel now on the road to recovery, I could concentrate on other things; I wanted to get my plan for murder moved along, I felt that I needed to get on with it, I needed to do something terrible in answer to something terrible happening to me.

I'm not a woman though, and multi-tasking is not a forte of mine, so although it could now be bought forward, thoughts of murder still had to remain behind looking after Mel, I wanted to make sure that she fully recovered before I started to put my efforts into murder.

Throughout the rest of the day Mell continued to make steps into recovery, and by the time evening came, I think she was pretty much over the hangover, and found that she was considering work the next day. I wasn't sure that was the best idea, but at least she was able to keep her cup of tea and a bowl of soup down. Which was progress.

By the time night time came I felt much more relaxed and at ease, it had been a tough few days, after a tough time, and I had been stressed. It looked like that was coming to an end though.

How wrong someone can be.

SEVENTY

With the arrival of the morning came the inevitable start of the working week, and expectedly and I think rightly, Mel said that she would stay off work today with the view to going in tomorrow.

It was a wonderful start to the day though, Mel was pretty much back to her usual self, she was very affectionate and my morning before having to leave was dosed heavily with kisses and hugs. This was something I could get used to.

When I went to step out of the house, Mel pulled me back from the doorway and hugged me, she didn't want to let me go, I hugged her back and we kissed passionately.

I promised her a slap up meal tonight when I got back from work, I planned to give our favourite Italian a call while I was at work and book us in for this evening. Seeing as Mel was now back on her feet and appeared to be over the alcohol, and although maybe not the tragedy, seemed to be ready to get on with things.

I gave her one last kiss before I left, I took hold of her hands and looked deep into her eyes; I told her I loved her and that everything would be ok, she smiled, a smile that I hadn't seen in a while and she nodded in agreement. She placed her forehead against mine, and whispered that she loved me too.

Our hands were the last to let go, both of us with our arms outstretched, as I headed to my car, this was what being in love with someone was all about. As I got into my car and put it into reverse, I couldn't take my eyes off her standing in the doorway. To me she was the most beautiful person I had ever seen, with morning hair, swathed only in a nightgown; she was stunning to me.

As I drove away I had the most amazing feeling of being in love, now to think about murder.

It was too early to contact the restaurant on the way to work, I'd have to do that from work a little later: I was sure there was no more wine in the house, so it would take a concerted effort for Mel to start drinking again, and besides, the way she had been this morning, I think she was past it and grateful.

So, after everything had happened recently I felt like things were coming back together; it wasn't easy, and believe me, the pain I felt at my loss, I figured that would remain with me, probably for the rest of my days.

I've heard people say it before, that you never fully get over a loss, but you adjust to take it into consideration and then get on with your life as best you can.

This was still early days for us, but after a little bit of a wobble, it looked like we were coming out the other side.

I could only imagine how people who had been left in the wake of my murders had been feeling, my loss was bad, and you can see what it did to Mel, but the loss of a loved one, someone you have nurtured throughout their lives, or someone you have come to depend on as being there to help bring up your children. Well, that must be an indescribable loss.

So you can see I'm not an emotionless robot or some kind of psychopath who enjoys killing, moreover that quite often murder is my necessity, to keep my from other things; but I would still need to kill someone and bring that loss onto someone else. It was unfortunate but I was starting to feel that way.

I felt that I owed it to Mel. As if there was a limited amount of loss in the world, and by making more and more people feel that loss, it would spread that loss thinner amongst those that felt it. Thereby Mel's feeling of loss would somehow be diminished.

See how my mind works? Everything is borne out of a necessity for something else.

SEVENTY ONE

It was a bit of an easy day at work. I had a meeting planned for the afternoon, but other than that and some of the usual bits of admin work, there wasn't a lot for me to do. Obviously I didn't say anything about that to anyone.

It gave me the ideal opportunity to put some thought into murder and at the same time organise a lovely meal with Mel for later in the evening.

As you know, I have an office at the end of a large open plan, and quite often I keep my door open, so anyone can just pop in and have a chat. Today though I wanted to concentrate, I needed to figure out some of the finer details, so I shut the door.

If anyone had just opened the door and come in, they would probably thought I had been asleep, I was relaxed in my chair, head resting against the back of the seat and I had my eyes closed. I wasn't sleeping, but it gave my mind more freedom to imagine things.

This is often how I came up with my plans, it was imagining it at first, and letting the potential issues come to light. It must have been a good way or sorting it out, as (touch wood) I had been undiscovered up until now. I wanted to make sure that the next one was absolutely no different.

I could use a tried and tested technique, as in do again something I had done before, but I was worried that it may somehow make me easier to identify, and that is something that cannot happen, let's face it, if I can get away with it this many times by going through this technique I can do it again.

Now I want to say, a lot has changed. You can see by the last one I have completely moved away from the gore of the first murder to the point where there was none. It was my personal preference as there are so many complications with the blood.

This one though, I kind of wanted the blood this time, in revenge for what had happened to me, this time I was going to have to prepare for the blood.

It was while I was thinking about the plan, and thinking about using that BMW, it made me think about the old Notebook house. I decided I'd put an application in via land registry, to see if I could find out who the current owners of the property were.

Sorry, I was flitting from one idea to another, almost like a brain storm, and one idea led me to think of something else. I never wrote anything down through, there could be no record of these kinds of thoughts.

I called up the restaurant and made the booking for 8pm.

I decided that I'd stop at a supermarket on the way home, I'd pick up some flowers to take back to Mel and a large sharp knife that I would need for the murder. I considered whether it should be a plunge type knife or a slit type knife; I suppose it would be better to see what they had before I made that decision.

Oh, I'd need a new pack of ibuprofen too, seeing as we had run out at home with my recurring migraine. I might even treat myself to some proper migraine relief instead of the super cheap generic own brand pain killers.

By the time I had had lunch and was going into the meeting, I had already sorted much of the stuff that I wanted to arrange for today. The meal was booked for later that evening, I had developed the outline for my next murder and had made steps into securing that Notebook house for us to develop and eventually move into.

It had been a productive day so far, now to get on with some boring work, I hated meetings; they were so dull.

SEVENTY TWO

I found it hard to keep my eyes open, there was very little that involved my department, and I had the answers for the small part that did. Most of the meeting was irrelevant to me and so keeping focus on what people was saying was difficult.

Plunge or slice? That was the question.

I didn't drift away thinking about that, I couldn't let myself; I didn't want to be guilty of any kind of Freudian slip while at work, I had to be careful.

My relief when they drew the meeting to a close was overwhelming, it was horrible being confined to things like this, especially when I was counting down the moment to be free and get back to Mel.

I was really looking forward to getting back.

There was still a little work to do before I could leave, but most of my working day was done, and the prospect of getting back was getting closer and closer.

I was counting down the minutes.

Anyway, with everything I needed to do done, it gave me a little longer to plan my murder. I'd chosen my target, obviously not the exact target, as those things were always a case of wrong place at the wrong time.

Still, I knew where I was going with it, I couldn't think of any reason why it would be a problem, witnesses would be at a minimum and I would be ready before I got there for the fallout in terms of blood and DNA.

I kind of want to give you the plan in advance, I mean it's not complete yet, and not everything is in place, but I almost want to give you something to look forward to, something you can expect to see coming your way soon.

With these ongoing thoughts the time flew by and it was finally time for me to clock out, which was exciting. I think I'd have to pop into Asda on the way home, just so that I could pick up those things we talked about earlier.

The short walk to my car was a relief, to be free from work for the rest of the day was great; I think the prospect of an appealing evening with Mel, especially after the recent run of events we'd had was such a good feeling that it had made the time I spent at work a real inconvenience. A necessity but an inconvenience all the same.

Still, it was over now and I could look forward to the evening.

I decided to go plunge while I was in Asda, and picked out an appropriate looking knife. It certainly looked like it would do the trick, it was quite a large meat knife of some sort; I'm no chef, so don't know the exact type, but the end of the knife was to a sharp point, and the blade was apparently razor sharp, and would never need sharpening.

It felt weighty and robust when I held it, and I liked the feel of the rubberised handle. It was the kind of knife you'd see in a horror movie, but in real life; and like the films it was going to be used to kill someone.

On the way home Heart FM was giving me a number of great tunes to sing along to, the flowers I picked up for Mel were on the passenger seat; I'd pulled off the label saying how much they were, and the receipt was in the bag with the knife, safe in the glovebox for now.

I pulled onto the drive and collected the flowers from the passenger seat.

SEVENTY THREE

I didn't need to hide the flowers behind my back, but I did.

When I walked in and closed the front door, there was no sign of Mel to start with, so I kept the flowers behind my back as I made my way into the kitchen, then the living room.

Nothing.

The kitchen was sparse too, as if she hadn't been using it; just like the days that she'd spent in bed, with the wine.

My heart sank, surely she hadn't delved back into that regime after the breakthrough we had had, she had appeared to back to her normal self this morning when I'd left.

I left the flowers in the kitchen, and with a heavy heart I made my way upstairs. There was no noise coming from upstairs and she clearly hadn't stirred by the noises of me coming home.

I just hoped she was sleepy, after an exhausting few days as opposed to be being back pissed again and in a slumber in the bed.

I didn't creep upstairs, I suppose in a bid to kind of give her some forewarning that I was coming up, or for the noises to break though the slumber and start to waken her.

Still nothing.

When I got to the bedroom, I found that the bed was made, and she was nowhere to be seen. Now this was turning into a little bit of a roller coaster, Scooby Doo style mystery.

I mean, I'd gone from being elated at arriving home, to my heart sinking that she had perhaps fallen back into her drunken regime, to a little bit of excitement again at the discovery that she wasn't drunk in bed.

There was the enigma of where she was though, the cottage wasn't big, and we'd never really played hide and seek before, so it's not like I was going to enter a room like the Pink Panther with Kato waiting to jump out on me.

It occurred to me that she may have gone out for a walk, then a horrible thought crossed my mind.

If she may have gone out for a walk, then she may have considered visiting the Notebook house, if she had considered visiting the Notebook house, then she would have discovered a BMW parked up on the long driveway.

Mel is conscientious and that's the kind of thing that she would report to the police, an abandoned car, on abandoned land.

Enter the roller coaster again, now my heart and mind was filled with thoughts of peril, the car would definitely link the murder in Wolverhampton to me, obviously they didn't know who I was, but it was another piece of the puzzle.

It would also ask questions from Mel, I mean, that Notebook house was almost overgrown, I'm not saying that we were the only two people in the world who knew it existed, but I was the only other person who Mel knew that knew about it.

I didn't want to think about Mel asking questions about a car involved in a murder, with me; I wasn't sure I'd got that good of a poker face for direct questions from Mel.

I could feel my migraine starting all of a sudden and I headed into the bathroom.

SEVENTY FOUR

I don't know why I keep heading back Wolverhampton way to commit my murders, it might be that it's my home town, and I know it well. In any case, my plan was to return to Wolverhampton, well just outside, Wednesfield to be exact.

I suppose in between Wednesfield and Wolverhampton to be precise, there's a small retail park, I can't really remember the name of it now, I know how to get there, but can't think what it's called.

Anyway, it's not really the retail park that interests me for my next murder, it's the canal system that runs around it.

There's quite a few canals in the West Midlands, I've heard there's more waterways around the West Midlands than in Venice, just not as scenic. This gave me an ideal place to commit my next murder.

When it comes to the canals and the road system there is an abundance of bridges, now link that with the retail park, which means there are people spending money; well, those that have it.

Then there's those that do not have it, and there are quite a few people around the area living rough, and you guessed it, one of these unfortunate souls was to be my next victim.

I suppose it's a hazard that goes with sleeping rough, you are at the risk of being vulnerable to almost anything while you sleep, even more so if you are a regular drug taker, and that sleep is even deeper.

So my plan was simple really, I'd wait until the early hours, obviously I'd need a plan to be staying out somewhere for Mel's benefit. Then I would walk the canals, and would assess the situation as I went.

I'd look primarily for a rough sleeper beneath one of the bridges, as it would make it a more secluded place, for both the discovery and any potential witnesses or CCTV.

When I found what I was after I would quite simply plunge the large knife into his neck, maybe more than once if necessity called for it, but I would be hoping the blade would damage the voice box from within as it passed making it as quiet as possible. There wasn't the potential for many witnesses, but didn't want to alert people all the same.

Obviously I'd need to be prepared for the blood, I could imagine there'd be a lot, and probably of the spurting type, if I caught the jugular that I was after. So I'd need as much disposable clothing as possible.

Something more to add to that every increasing bundle of evidence in the boot of the BMW. I'd probably have to torch that poor old car at some point.

The thought of torching that trusty BMW probably filled me with more regret than the thought of plunging the knife into some innocent guy's throat. How that's possible I don't know, but there you go.

I think the word is callous.

Maybe about some things, but not everything. As you already know. Anyway with all this talk about murder I've kind of digressed from the task at hand and that was trying to work out where on Earth Mel had gone.

Hopefully it wasn't the Notebook house, as that might bring up questions and discoveries, which might mean I lose my mode of transport for the next murder, which again would be a shame.

SEVENTY FIVE

To see her hanging there, behind the bathroom door, was probably more than my brain was able to process. I stood there, frozen, looking at the sight in front of me. My eyes unable to close to protect me from the truth, barely able to take a breath.

Her eyes were open and her tongue filled the gap of her mouth between her teeth, it looked swollen; there was a line of dried blood on the very edge of both her top and bottom lip where they met the tongue.

She had both arms at her side, and her legs outstretched. Her bottom was raised off the floor, her neck taking the weight of her body.

I was surprised to see the cord from her dressing gown had taken the weight without either slipping or breaking, not that she was heavy, I don't know, it didn't seem a capable thing, but it was.

She had trapped one end of the cord against the top of the door to the bathroom and the doorframe. There was part of the cord sticking out the landing side of the door, but I'd not seen it.

The other end was tied around her neck, there were indentations on her neck where it was biting into the skin and flesh, and where most of her weight was being held; the skin around the cord had started to turn a blueish colour, like the forming of a deep bruise.

I'll probably never be able to forget her eyes looking at me in this way, her head was to one side, almost over her left shoulder, with her makeshift noose making her look up at me; and that's how I'll always remember seeing her last.

I don't know how long I was stood there, I completely lost track of time. It wasn't like there was any chance of life within her and I needed to act quickly to save her.

She was dead.

For the second time in my life, and from out of nowhere, my heart broke out of my mouth with a scream. I want to say it was an elongated scream of the single word 'no', but I can't be sure, something came out, and the fact that it was screamed is probably all I can definitely say.

I can't describe to you the instant and overwhelming feeling of loss, I was never going to wake up next to this lovely woman again. She was never going to sit next to me on the sofa and cuddle me, I was never going to be able to tell her how much I love her.

A million moments ran through my head, of Christmases now lost in time, birthdays uncelebrated; sharing summer holidays away, and even just the simple pleasure of holding her hand around the supermarket. Gone.

Life can change in the blink of an eye, I've seen that first hand, but the unescapable truth, in that Mel was never going to be near me again, broke my heart; not only broke it but all life, love and happiness spilled from the splits into the empty void in my chest.

My heart in this way, not the beating physical blood pump, but the excitement filled emotional, loving and warm element of what we call the heart; well, that was a shrivelled black, drained and empty container now. I felt everything drain from it, I was broken, to the degree that I was unfixable. The damage of what I was seeing had on me, was something I could never overcome.

I was lost.

As my emotionless sense of loss and foreboding encompassed me I all of a sudden wondered what I should do. She was dead, beyond doubt, should I call an ambulance or what? My mind, struggling to cope with the most basic of thoughts, couldn't cope.
When I dialled 999 and they asked me what service, I just said that I didn't know and that my girlfriend had killed herself.

Ambulance and the police turned up some time later, it could have been minutes or an hour or more, I was so lost in myself time didn't register.

I wanted to hug her, I wanted to hold her to my chest, whisper that I loved her into her ear and hear her gasp an intake of breath; I wanted to kiss her, cradle her and never let her go.

As the tears welled up in my eyes, and the doorbell rang, it was with a sense of that my life would never be the same again that I opened the door.

The ambulance crew rushed upstairs and freed her from her deathly restraint, they placed her on a monitor that only confirmed what they could already see for themselves, her heart wasn't beating; the paramedic confirmed life extinct.

Life extinct, that was two words that meant a whole lot to me, I just never thought I'd hear them like this. Never did I think that I'd hear those words in reference to my Mel, well not for a good 40 years or so.

My tears were rolling down my face, I wasn't crying as such, but the tears came all the same. The police examined her body and filled in a report for the coroner, there were no suspicious circumstances, and they consoled me for my loss. They had no idea of my loss, Mel was not just another dead body, she had been the embodiment of everything that I loved.

With her dead, only a lonely, loveless existence awaited me. Now I knew how they felt, the ones I'd made suffer with what I had done. Now I knew fully, the loss of a walking, smiling, loving individual who was full of life.

It was the kind of heart breaking that I'm unable to describe to you. I'd like to think that I've given you a feeling for what my life has been like. This however, this is something I can't adequately explain. The devil here is completely in the detail.

I would miss Mel in every aspect of my life, nothing I ever did would now ever amount to what it could have been if I had done it with Mel.

There was now an ever present void that couldn't be filled. All of her little nuances, the way her mouth curled at the one corner when she smiled, the way she flicked her hair from her face, the tone of her voice, all of those things only existed now as a memory. I could hear her talk in my head, but that was the only place that I was ever going to hear it again.

It was all of these unaccountable things that were the hardest to lose, the little things, the things I would change anything for, to see, hear and hold again.

Things moved on with only limited input from me, the undertaker soon arrived and before I knew it she was with them and off to the mortuary.

As I closed the door, the real realisation hit me that I was closing the door and Mel would never walk through it again. I was holding the card from the funeral director, so I knew where she had gone, but all of a sudden I realised that I had actually let her go, let her leave without holding, or kissing her, and that opportunity would never present itself again.

I cursed myself for being in such a dreamlike trance and allowing it to happen, but that's exactly what it had been like. I'd acknowledged things, people and decisions from a distant part of my psyche, like I was looking out of my eyes, but they were binoculars the wrong way around; everyone was far away, the sounds of their voices understandable but muffled.

Now came the emptiness.

It was deafening, it felt like pressure on my ears against my head. The silence and lifelessness of the house all of a sudden made it feel unwelcoming and uncomfortable.

There was a life once lived here that was now lost. Over half of the things that were in this house were as a result of Mel, the clothes, some of the food, a whole shelf in the bathroom. There were a million little things that were now redundant.

Worthless.

Meaningless.

I walked into the kitchen and put the kettle on, I was going to have to call her mom and dad, mine too.

To add insult to injury, my stress headache started to encroach and I could feel one of those migraines coming on. I should get that checked out, I heard Mel say in my head.

I promised I would.

SEVENTY SIX

My parents were around in what seemed like a flash, I wept on their shoulders, unabashed and uncontrollably.

They just hugged me in silence and let me cry, there were no words that they could say that could take my pain away, they knew and I knew. So they were just there for me to hold onto.

Once I was able to maintain a degree of composure I asked them if they wanted a drink, but my mom made us all a cup of tea.

In the end they convinced me to go with them and stay at their house for the night, they would bring me back tomorrow, when Mel's parents were going to come. I have to say I wasn't looking forward to that, not that I had done anything wrong, they knew I loved Mel, it was just going to be a horror show of emotion.

Being back in the room I grew up in, seemed oddly comforting, it was my old single bed still, but when I got in it, I went straight to sleep.

When I woke up I had a terrifying feeling that I couldn't work out where I was, I couldn't work out where the door or window was, and it took me a second to realise I was at my parents.

Then the pain of losing her hit me again. There was no escape.

I still couldn't believe it had happened, it was harder to believe that I'd never see her again. It was remembering her in the most mundane of moments that were hardest to reconcile, just wandering around the house, walking through the door after work, those type of things.

My brain couldn't accept it was forever, it kind of expected the dream to be over at some point and I'd be back with her and everything would be alright.

It was never ever going to be the same.

My parents took me back home, obviously I had to call work and tell them what had happened, they simply said take as much time as I needed.

What I needed was to stab one of the rough sleepers in the neck in the middle of the night; that was what I needed, now more than ever.

I didn't know, as I'd not been in this position but I was sure that to put my plan of killing a homeless person into action might help alleviate some of the pain I felt over Mel, perhaps replace that emotion with other emotions.

I know what you're thinking, this sparks an absolute murderous rampage in me, well, you'll have to wait and see won't you.

I was right about Mel's parents, when they turned up they were as inconsolable as me, we were all crying together.

Strangely her dad thanked me, he said he knew how happy I'd made her and how much she loved me. He said, that Mel had been his reason for living, he had been born and placed on the planet to be her father and bring her up; protect her, nurture her, give her the things she needed and some of the things she wanted. He loved her without question, he would have laid down his life for her; if he could swap places with her he would.

Mel clearly meant everything to him, I'm not sure who was feeling the greatest loss. Not that it was a competition, but I could see the man was as broken as I was.

We talked about the funeral, and the arrangements, I was happy for her to go back up north to be with the rest of her family, and that meant a lot to them, she was their daughter after all. They took a couple of mementos from the house when they left.

This was going to be the first time I was going to be on my own in what I considered to be our house, I heard Mel tell me that it would be ok, that she'd help me through it and that she would always be with me.

I cracked open my bottle of Captain Morgan and mixed a large glass of it with some cola. I disliked the taste of wine, I was sticking with the Cap'n for the night.

SEVENTY SEVEN

My headache was unbearable, not my stress headache, this was too much of the Captain. I felt sick too, I decided to try the hair of the dog, and turned back to the Captain for a respite from the headache and nausea.

I'd never really tried the hair of the dog before, but it seemed to do the trick, the only problem was by 10a.m the rest of the bottle was gone.

I strolled down to the local shop and picked up another bottle, more expensive than a supermarket, but I wanted not to step into soberness and endure that pain for a while, there was too much pain going on for me to be bothered with a hangover.

One necessity leads to another. Maslow said something similar I'm sure.

I can't remember if there was football on the TV or the Grand Prix, but I finished that bottle of Captain Morgan and went and got another.

I kind of knew in myself that I shouldn't continue drinking, but I didn't like the alternative, it sort of numbed my pain, and the emptiness Mel left in me.

Don't get me wrong, I was talking to Mel all of the time, she was even commentating on the tackles, if it was football I'd been watching, and she never used to do that.

The day seemed to roll on past me, I didn't bother going to bed, I lay out on the sofa instead, it was easier for the TV and the continued Captain Morgan, the only problem was the toilet, so I started to piss into the empty Captain Morgan bottle, it saved the number of journeys upstairs.

In the end, I don't know whether I had been drinking for a day or two, I'd kind of lost track of the time. I hadn't charged my phone, and didn't care that I hadn't spoken to anyone.

I went upstairs and emptied the bottles of piss and took the liberty of having a piss myself. I was unsteady on my feet, and I could start to feel the budding hangover starting to raise its ugly head.

I was out of cash, and the shop didn't take cards, so I was stuck on what to do. Wait out the hangover or risk going to the supermarket, it was a drive away, but not a far drive. I was confident I could make it there and back, I mean I'd never seen a policeman or police car in all the times I'd driven there.

In my mind it was rational, I needed the alcohol, driving was the only realistic and civilised way of getting there, I was drunk, but it's easier to sit down and drive than walk.

There was no option really.

I emptied the last dregs out of the glass, it was literally a tiny amount, less than a sip and went and got my keys.

When I went outside the air hit me and I took a deep breath of that beautiful air, It filled my lungs and made my body sway, I think I took a few steps away from where I wanted to go, my drunkenness not helping.

Sitting in the driver's seat I felt comfortable, it felt natural and easy, I felt in myself that I wasn't fit enough to drive, and shouldn't really. It was just I was sure loads of people did it, and I was sure it was something I could get away with just this once.

I sat there for a second looking at the passenger seat, Mel had been in that seat so many times, it was her seat.

It was empty, and I cried again.

SEVENTY EIGHT

It felt dreamy as I drove towards the supermarket, it was like the headlights and street lights were passing in a blur, it took all of my concentration to watch the car in front and brake when I needed to.

There are a lot of things I've done that I don't agree with, and this is one of them.

My need for another bottle of Captain Morgan outweighed my morals in relation to drink driving though, justified.

As I pulled perfectly into a parking space, I sat back and relaxed, it had been a bit of a terrifying ordeal getting there, and I was on the edge of my nerves; the good thing though was that I had survived. I got out and made my way in, I decided that I'd get a couple of bottles while I was on to save future trips like this.

It wasn't very busy as I staggered my way around the supermarket, don't get me wrong, I wasn't falling over things but I was unsteady I suppose more than staggering.

I'd picked myself up a basket and placed a couple of large bottles of Captain Morgan into it, I also selected a couple of large bottles of cola too. Then I was hit with a brainwave, I'd get a bag of ice cubes too.

Mel gave me a mental high five at my awesomeness.

Before I knew it I was back in the car, taking a deep breath before I dared my perilous journey back home. Perhaps a quick sip would settle my nerves, and it did.

I felt a renewed confidence in my ability, and despite my car actually taking up two parking spaces, I was resolute that my driving skill could only have been improved by the alcohol.

They say that a third of all car accidents are caused by drink drivers, which means that two thirds of accidents are caused by people who are sober. Well, surely it's safer to drive while you're drunk by those statistics.

Anyway, I was back behind the wheel and was best part home, I felt a feeling of relief as I pulled onto the estate, I had done it. It had been worth the risk after all, now I could while away the next few hours in front of the TV and delve deeper and deeper into my stupor.

This was exactly what was needed for now, I couldn't bear the thought of facing up to my feelings about Mel, and this had done me proud so far.

As the car reversed off the driveway, I couldn't believe what I was seeing. Didn't they think to check the road before pulling some kind of manoeuvre like that? What kind of idiots were...

My car made an almighty bang as it caught the rear quarter of their car, even drunk time seemed to slow down for me, I saw the metal of my bonnet crumple up obscuring my view out of the windscreen, and I was immediately buffered and shunted in my seat. The entire aftermath took place in slow motion, but in fact must have only taken a second, maybe two seconds at the most; It didn't feel like that at the time though.

As the air bag exploded out of the steering wheel, with what looked like some kind of fiery talc, it burned the inside of my forearms, it actually grazed them with the ferocity of the explosion.

I hadn't been expecting a car to pull out like this, and my brain went into complete panic, I tried to brake, but it was the accelerator and the car revved and raced, it sped up with a lurch at the sudden rush of petrol into the engine and flew against the rear of their car, scraping along the nearside of mine, pulling off their rear bumper and a whole load of bodywork from my doors. Their car spinning around against the kerb.

I could hear my tyres brushing against the crumpled bodywork.

It made me think of the days we used to stick a squashed drinks can in between the brake callipers of our bikes when I was a kid. The can rubbed on the ridges of the tyre and made it sound like a car engine. This sound was more like a chainsaw.

As my battered car gathered speed across the road, the glance against the rear of their car had diverted my direction, and I was now careering into the back of another car parked on someone else's drive.

Again the sound as the two cars collided was deafening, there was the sound of breaking glass and grinding metal, and I was thrown all over the place in my seat; I was like a rag doll, I was at the complete mercy of inertia. It was lucky my seat belt was on.

I'd hit my head against the side window, before the glass smashed into a thousand pieces; there was blood on the airbag from my nose, I could feel wetness running down the side of my head.

I didn't really feel any pain, at the time.

I'd lost all control and any thought of either steering or braking had gone from my mind, leaving me in the position that I was at the mercy of the car, my foot came off the accelerator in the madness of being thrown around.

I realised the car was now at least at rest, there was smoke coming from the engine and the tyres, and all of a sudden I was hit with the fear that the car was on fire.

I did not want to be trapped in a car that was on fire.

The crash had created complete clarity and I was all of a sudden stone cold sober, I didn't feel drunk in the slightest.

At the thought of burning alive, I undid my seatbelt and opened my door, but the door didn't open; the crunched and crumpled metal, bent and warped misshapen frame of the door prevented any movement, it gave a creak sound as the metal gave a little but nothing moved to the degree I could get out.

Panic again.

SEVENTY NINE

As I sat in the driver's seat feeling trapped, a distant voice came to me. It said I was going to get out, I was going to be ok. It wasn't Mel talking it was someone else, it was someone outside.

My ears were ringing, and my head was fuzzy; a mix of the alcohol, the injury and the violent shaking it had undergone. My right ear especially felt as if it was full, and the sounds coming through it were muffled, if anything was getting through at all.

I was staring at the woman standing outside my car, and it was her who was talking to me, there was no glass in my door window but her voice still sounded like she was talking to me through double glazing.

She went to the back door of my car, driver's side; which must have been fairly unscathed as it opened and she leaned into the car to talk to me and see if I could get out. I could smell burning, and burnt rubber, and had a horrible feeling that the car was about to explode. Like it would do in a film.

I moved my legs, there wasn't any pain, and everything seemed ok. My arms hurt on the inside from the airbag, but I'd got strength in them, nothing seemed broken. I twisted in my seat and clambered into the back of the car.

It was pretty much like climbing into the front after committing murder, but in reverse, I sprawled out in the back seat and came out of the car head first.

The woman was talking to me, but I couldn't really take in anything she was saying, it was just dull noise. I looked at the scene.

My car was a wreck, the door I'd clambered out of was probably the only door that was capable of being used. The rest of the car was a crumpled mess that didn't really look like my car; the bumper was hanging off at the front, one of the headlights was missing altogether, and the bonnet looked like the BFG had held it too tight in his hand, it was odd to see metal folded like that.

I surveyed the carnage, see what I did there? Car..nage.. of the wider situation.

The car I'd parked into had been shunted against the house, it think the glass in the porch was smashed, and the rear of that car was as unsightly to look at as mine.

I hadn't been travelling very fast and was amazed at the amount of damage I'd been able to cause. My hands were shaking and this woman wouldn't stop talking to me, trying to get me to sit down. I really didn't want to sit down.

The car which had stupidly reversed off the drive without looking, had been turned 90 degrees and was now parallel against the pavement, it could have been parked, except for the great swathe of dented bodywork and exposed bare metal.

Thankfully everyone was ok, I reassured Mel that I was fine, and held my hand up to the side of my head, I saw that there was blood on my hand but it didn't look too bad, let's face it I'd seen a nasty head injury on Emma Jackson, this was nothing like that.

Considering the amount of damage, the fact that I was standing up and relatively unharmed amazed me, it sure showed the importance of those collision tested crumple zones.

As the sirens got closer, and the blue lights started reflecting on the buildings, the consequences started to materialise. This hadn't been my fault, there was no way this could be construed as being my fault, other than the fact that I was probably two times over the drink drive limit.

The thought that I needed to run away came too late, as the ambulance and the police pulled around the corner. I was fucked.

EIGHTY

Now you might think, that as a guy who has eluded the police for some considerable time, having committed the most horrendous of acts; that escaping the police over something as trivial as a car accident would be child's play.

Like everything though, it depends upon your frame of reference.

Despite how it appears I'm not a career criminal and those urges and the autonomic desire to escape isn't written into my DNA, and certainly isn't a learned trait.

It is only my considered scheming and planning that has kept me out of custody, so this unexpected debacle, having thrust itself on me took me completely by surprise. Suffice to say I wasn't prepared, I certainly wasn't prepared for what was to come.

Anyway, like I say, when the police arrived my thoughts of fleeing were already too late.

Even the sound of the sirens were muffled through my right ear, and the as the ambulance approached, it ceased the sirens but kept the blue lights on. The ambulance stopped short of the wreckage in the road and blocked the road off so that no other cars could involve themselves in the accident.

I walked towards the ambulance and saw the police car directly behind it, this adopted a similar position in the road, its blue lights still on.

The paramedics were quickly off the ambulance and approached me. Instead of getting anything off the ambulance they held my arm and walked me to the ambulance, the opened the back door and I climbed inside.

As the rear door closed I saw the police officers surveying the scene.

The ambulance crew put me in a neck brace and sat me down on a seat adjacent to the stretcher. They were asking me questions and started examining my injury to the side of my head.

To be honest, I know they put a neck brace on, probably out of precaution, but I didn't really feel in any pain, certainly not from my neck.

Maybe the fact that my blood contained a significant amount of Captain Morgan helped.

As my adrenaline started to ebb away and be replaced by shock, my drunkenness started to return and I started shaking.

The paramedics tended to the injury to the side of my head, and applied a bandage, which they tied tight. They then took my blood pressure and monitored my heart rate, by hooking me up to a machine that automatically tightened up a blood pressure cuff on my left arm, and a small clip with a red light on my finger.

They then surveyed my other injuries, on my forearms from the airbag and, released the neck brace to examine my movement and any pain in my neck. There was none and they left the neck brace off.

There was a knock on the door of the ambulance, and without really waiting for an answer, the door was opened by a tall slim policeman, who climbed into the back.

He gave me an acknowledging look, then talked about me in the third person to the ambulance crew.

He was asking how I was doing, what my injuries were and whether I was likely to go to hospital. The paramedic turned from me to talk to him, and raised his right hand to his mouth as if holding an invisible glass, in a gesture that simulated drinking.

The policeman raised his eyebrows and got off the ambulance

again.

It was when the police officer returned, clutching a small device in his hand, that I started to develop a sense of dread.

I was in a situation that I couldn't escape from, I was trapped. It was a horrible feeling, knowing what is about to happen, and that it's something you don't want to have to go through; yet having no control over it at all.

I wanted to just stand up and say that I was drunk, let's just get on with it; but I didn't, I just sat there and awaited the impending doom.

I sat there thinking about that stupid Captain Morgan and the hangover I was trying to avoid, how things were going to have to change from here on in.

How was I going to cope without my car?

EIGHTY ONE

Make no mistake, this was going to be a shit sandwich, and I was going to have to take a massive bite, maybe even swallow.

I mean, I could cope with a fine, but if this ended up in a driving ban, it was going to change everything. How would I get to work? Any thought of murder would have to be put on hold. Well, it might mean I'd have to execute that poor soul under the bridge sooner rather than later; but on the whole it would alter everything.

When the paramedic said that I wouldn't need to go to hospital, I think I put my head in my hands. To be fully open with you, going to hospital had crossed my mind as an avenue out of this mess, but with those few words he destroyed any hope of that.

This left me to the mercy of the police, and to be fair I don't think mercy is in their vocabulary. The paramedics stood aside completing their paperwork, and the policeman pressed between them, he sat on the stretcher opposite me.

He was talking to me, but I don't really remember exactly what he was saying to be honest, I seem to remember I felt like he was arresting me straight off, without even doing anything and before he had even put the white plastic tube on top of the device he'd been holding.

I was watching him, he hadn't even asked my name, and was talking while he was working the device, he didn't bother to look at me and I was starting to get infuriated, not by the fact that I was busted, but his demeanour.

We both knew that my breathing into it was a formality, and no doubt if he wanted to, he could actually have arrested me straight away.

Anyway, I followed his instructions and blew through the tube, I'm not asthmatic or anything, but I did feel like I was reaching my blowing limit before the thing beeped to tell me I could stop.

Everything was still dreamy, and despite what the ambulance crew had said about me not needing to go to hospital, I had quite the headache, and the sounds through my ear were still muffled. I wasn't really suffering any other pain though, perhaps it's one of those 'you'll feel that in the morning' things.

FAIL.

Of course it was, I couldn't feign surprise and neither could he, it was with a mundanely resolute attitude that he arrested me and put the handcuffs on.

I stood up and as I did so, took a mighty step forward without intention, this was a proper stumble and acted as proof of my drunkenness, as if any was needed. If I said anything and I can't remember that I did, it would have come out slurred without question.

The policeman held me tightly beneath my left elbow as he walked me to his car, I was concentrating hard on keeping my equilibrium; I didn't want to come across as drunk as I was and it was almost as if me concentrating on it was making it worse. I was all over the place.

I was cursing myself for being unable to control such a simple thing as walking, clearly by this time my adrenaline was completely exhausted and the full extent of my drunkenness was starting to shine through.

Then to add insult to injury I started to hiccup. How embarrassing.

EIGHTY TWO

After nearly ten minutes of hiccups, with the pain on the diaphragm you've either experienced or not, I did the only thing that can possibly cure them, I fell asleep. Can you believe it? Arrested, drunk, hands cuffed together, in the back of a police car, I fell asleep; and no doubt snored.

The rear door being opened awoke me from my slumber, the policeman actually said something funny to me as I woke up, but for the life of me I can't remember what he said now. I remember laughing to myself inside, I tried my best to keep it in, which probably ended up in a weird looking smile.

He helped me out of the car and again, I did the stupid concentrate on the walking thing, and stumbled my way through a series of heavy steel doors.

He sat me down on a bench in a small room, until he was waived through to speak to the man behind the desk.

Talk about questions, Jesus Christ there were loads of questions, I was tired, I was drunk and all I really wanted to do was go to sleep. I didn't want to be rude but I was falling asleep while the guy behind the desk was asking me questions.

It was all very formal, if I'm honest I was in a state where I couldn't quite grasp everything that was happening and going on, I was agreeing with stuff and signing things, and to be fair and honest I didn't really know what I was doing.

I was eventually led through into a small room with the proper breathalyser, I mean this thing took up half of the rear wall, I don't remember much but the thing I took from this little episode was that this machine was precise and would tell them exactly how much I'd had to drink.

By this time I was past really caring, I just wanted to do what I needed to do to get myself some sleep. In reality the last thing I

241

actually wanted was sleep, with sleep would come soberness and that came hand in hand with hangover. I did not want to experience hangover at all.

Obviously I don't know it right now, but my potential hangover is not the thing I should be worrying about, but like I've said before and will say again, hindsight is a fantastic thing; yet less useful than a chocolate teapot.

I don't really see the point in going through every single detail of what happened to me through this little episode of my life. Like most things I've talked about so far, you'll either be able to associate with what is going on or you won't. If you've never been arrested and been in a police cell, well it's a hard thing to describe; if you have you'll know what I'm talking about.

I went through the procedure, and no miracles happen, I blow well over the limit. I still have it somewhere I'm sure, a receipt telling me exactly how much alcohol was in my breath. Like the numbers or anything on it really means anything to me.

The most important thing to me right at the time was trying to go and get some sleep, so I'm just following the policeman around, doing as he says when he tells me to do it and doing whatever I can to bring that bed and sleep closer.

Everything is documented and precise, it's very formal and I can imagine there's a written script for everything that goes on. Please let me sleep.

Now something very important happens right here, it's not something I was completely expecting, and not something I really knew was going to happen. Let's go beyond that, there a couple of important things going to happen here, and as we go on you'll see what I'm talking about; the first one happens pretty much straight away.

EIGHTY THREE

My eyes are so tired I can't tell you how hard it is to keep them open. If I was just tired it would have been easier, and let's be honest, sober in a police custody block would have kept me awake in itself. I'm drunk though, so sleep seems like a totally natural thing to do.

I was standing next to the policeman at the desk and was asked to sign in a few boxes on a piece of paper, for my belongings etc as I was going to be staying with them for a while. No shit.

Now the next bit didn't really sink in until a little later.

One of the boxes I had signed for was for them to take my fingerprints, photograph and DNA, I had signed it without any kind of thought going into it. Well thoughts of sleep perhaps.

I was told that I could get some sleep straight after documentation was done, which wouldn't take long, this was absolute music to my ears.

These were the last few things I needed to do, so I steeled myself and prepared for another half hour or so before sleep.

The room was like a small examination room, there was a photo booth, like the kind of thing that you'd see in a supermarket for your passport photograph; which of course I had to sit in for them to take my mug shot. I didn't have to hold a board up with my name on it in front of a height chart like I was kind of expecting.

There was also a machine linked up to a computer, this was pretty impressive. When someone said fingerprints, I was thinking black ink, and prints on a piece of paper; now I think about it properly that is probably stuff from the old films rather than anything recent.

No, this machine read the fingerprints like a barcode scanner, I

243

placed my fingers and hand on it and it read them like a photocopier; to be honest if I wasn't both drunk and in trouble, I would probably have been really impressed by it. At the time though, it was just one thing closer to sleep.

A quick swab on the inside of my mouth and I was in a cell. I even had my own toilet.

The bed, was a blue plastic covered uncomfortable mattress; if you could call it that. It was more like a mat to do gymnastics on, than something to get comfy and sleep on. The mattress was slung on top of a raised shelf, no more than 4 inches off the floor; obviously no-one wanted me inured if I fell out of bed.

I didn't care though, pretty much as soon as I was down on it I was asleep.

Whether it was because I was uncomfortable, or cold, or that the Captain Morgan was starting to wear off, but I didn't stay asleep very long.

It could have been that the words and their meaning had penetrated the veil of mist over my conscious mind, and things that had been said started to register with it.

It wasn't the first thing I thought of when I woke, the first thing I thought of was that my neck was stiff. The second was probably the ache behind my eyes to the back of my head, as that hangover headache encroached.

Mix into the equation that I was becoming nauseous, the words that may have woke me up were still not yet to the forefront of my mind.

I could tell I was going to be sick, there was this feeling in my jaw if that's possible, like the jaw itself was secreting saliva, and that saliva was collecting at the back of my mouth. I swallowed hard a few times to try and keep everything in and down, but clearly my body didn't want that.

I looked at the toilet which seemed to add some sort of urgency to my desire to be sick, almost as if seeing the toilet made any prospect of avoiding being sick impossible.

I quickly crawled over to the toilet on all fours, as my brain decided this would be the quickest and simplest way to get there.

Now you've been sick, and you know, even after it's all done there's still that desire to wretch; I hate that.

Now the nausea only added to my headache, you can see where this is going, a full blown hangover, and with how much I had drunk, over the period of time I had done so, this one was going to be spectacular.

I was holding the back of my head for comfort, and there was a genuine fear that should I move it too quickly it was prone to cracking, the pain was so fierce from it. I tried rubbing my forehead but this only gave momentary relief.

If I'd have been in any other situation I would probably have sworn to myself never to drink again, as I had already done in the past; but I wasn't in a normal situation and instead I was cursing myself for being so stupid.

This was without any doubt one of the worst hangovers I had ever had, possibly anyone had ever had; and I had subjected myself to more than quite a few of them in the past, so could base my consideration on fact.

This situation was the exact thing I was trying to avoid when I started this stupid drink driving endeavour, now I had to endure it without the comforts of my own home. Still, I suppose, this cell was as empty as home without Mel there.

To add to everything the pangs of loneliness hit me. What else could go wrong?

EIGHTY FOUR

Shit loads is the answer you're looking for, and if you said that then you'd be right. I had no idea sitting there nursing my insignificant hangover how totally shit things could go. I mean, right there I was thinking that sitting in a cell with a hangover, having lost Mel and Jamie Millie, was about as low as it could go. If only, if only it were and things were different; they're not though and there a whole new world consisting of many levels of shit left beyond what I thought was possible.

After three or so hours of pacing around the cell, clutching my head and pressing the button hoping someone would come and check on me, I was still all alone. I saw someone come to a small window in the door every now and then, but as soon as I said anything they were gone, not to return for ages.

After a long time I did manage to get a cup of coffee. It came straight back up, wasted.

They asked me if I wanted breakfast at one point, but the thought of eating anything made me even more nauseous, I begrudgingly took a Frosties cereal bar to keep for later.

Now pacing around a cell, wondering what is happening and what is going to happen is not a nice place to be. If you haven't been there, I honestly suggest avoiding it if at all possible.

I'm not saying there wasn't anyone looking after me, but looking back I think bearing in mind I had been involved in a significant car accident, they perhaps should have been checking in through that little window in the door more often.

In any case it's done now and doesn't matter.

So, anyway, pacing around the cell, whether it was a mixture of the alcohol withdrawal, the hangover, the lack of food, muscles tightening after the crash; whatever it was, my headache was fierce.

246

I decided I needed to have a lie down and try and take the weight off my head, rest it against the mattress.

I think that this was my body's way of getting me into a position that would cause the least amount of damage.

Before I could lie down properly, I collapsed.

I think for some of the time I must have been unconscious, because I don't remember anything at all, it's like being asleep. However there are other times that I can hear what is going on and what people are saying, I just can't open my eyes or move.

The next thing I really know is that I can hear people talking about me, they are close, almost right next to me, but it's dark, I can't open my eyes and all I can really hear is the panic in their tone. I don't know how long I'd been unconscious.

What I couldn't understand to start with was the talk about the blood.

I wasn't in pain, not that I could feel anything, but they were shouting to ring for an ambulance and were trying to see where the blood was from. I was wondering if I'd hurt myself as I went to lay down or something.

By the time the ambulance arrived I had managed to get my eyes open, various staff, both police and ambulance were asking me questions, and I was doing my best to reply, but I could hear myself slurring the words as I was trying to talk.

In the end I gave up, I was constantly being asked to repeat what I was saying and I could hear what was coming out of my mouth in my own ears, it was nonsense, but I couldn't change the slur no matter what, so I gave up trying to say anything.
Before long I was on a stretcher, and with police either side of me was being taken to hospital.

This is not where I escape. Just so you know, this is not a daring ploy to gain early freedom, I'm not going to make a break for the Mexican border.

No, this is what I mean when I'm talking about my insignificant hangover, this is something else.

EIGHTY FIVE

By the time we arrive at hospital I'm starting to feel a little more lucid, I've got a degree of control back over my mouth, but along with the regain of control comes the return of the headache.

The blood it seems has come from my nose, so I must've hurt my nose on the way down as I collapsed, and it has nothing at all do with either the accident or the hangover.

During all of the commotion I seemed to have come out of the other side of my hangover mostly. I was starting to feel much better and was gutted to have left my Frosties bar back in the cell.

After about an hour or so at hospital, I had managed to sit myself up and was actually feeling quite good.

The police officers who were looking after me said that I should have been kept handcuffed, but I seemed ok and that as long as I didn't start to 'play up' they'd keep them off. Obviously my mind turned instantly to escape.

I don't escape, you already know that, but believe me, as soon as I knew the cops were taking it easy on me, and they didn't think I'd do anything, I immediately started thinking about it. These two policemen had absolutely no idea what I was capable of.

Kill two policemen? I'm not Jason Bourne, they wouldn't be expecting me to do anything, and I suppose they were a little vulnerable, but not enough for something like that. They'd know who I was then.

Those words rang around my head like a bell.

By this time all of the dreaminess that comes with drunkenness had evaporated, and despite everything that had happened to me this morning, my mind was back to working quite well.

It hit me all of a sudden and the impact made my heart jump, and sent it straight up my chest into my mouth, before falling back down into a black pit, a sinking feeling engulfed me as my heart returned to its resting place.

A simple sentence came back to me; the DNA sample will be subject to a speculative search. A speculative search, holy shit I was fucked.

It's hard to describe the impact these words had on me now that I was sober and could understand what they meant properly.

If I thought I'd had feelings of dread before that was nothing in comparison to this. I didn't know how long it was going to take, but at some point soon, everything I had done was going to come out.

There was no way around it at all, they already had the sample; that swab inside my mouth when I was desperate for sleep. That tiny little swab was going to ruin everything, that tiny little swab was at some point going to stick me in jail for a long time.

I started to wonder how long it would take for a result, I mean, would they get it back while I was still here? Would it take weeks or months? There were a lot of unknown elements that made my thoughts about it divert onto thousands of tangents. The number of what ifs I came up with over the next couple of hours was incredible.

If the policemen saw me shuffling around uncomfortably on my bed, then they may have thought I was suffering from some sort of physical discomfort as opposed to being tortured by my mind.

EIGHTY SIX

The doctor that examined me asked me questions about what
had happened and why. I was kind of hoping that he would be
able to give me some of those answers, I neither knew what had
happened or why it had happened.

He shone his torch in my eyes, listened to my chest, he
examined my ears and the other age old associated doctor tests
you can imagine. In the end he said he'd have a look what was
going on inside and see if there was anything going on relating
to the accident.

I knew it really, I had done something during the crash that had
been missed by the ambulance crew, if I had been bleeding
down my nose like they said, it could be something quite
serious.

My emotions were all over the place now, I mean, I had the
impending doom of the DNA, mixed in with fear that I'd injured
something serious inside; link all that with the loss and the
murders, I was starting to lose my grip on it all.

I'd done so well keeping everything together over the years, it
was hard to think that it was all starting to unravel, and I was
unable to do anything about it. I felt trapped and helpless.

Everything takes an age in hospital, there's so much waiting
around. I was grateful though, I mean, bearing in mind the
treatment I was getting, it wasn't going to cost me an extra
penny. I paid every month, but when I needed to use it, it was
there, slow but there.

Before I knew they were wheeling me down the corridors for a
CT scan. The police following behind the bed. I laughed to
myself, not so long ago I was following one of their colleagues
around waiting on him to make the decisions, now it was their
turn to follow me around.

I lay there and considered whether I should say something, whether I should just come out with everything I had done to one of those policemen watching me.

I wondered what they'd say, whether they would believe me or not.

Now I wouldn't say that I'm claustrophobic. I'm not keen on tight spaces, and the thought of going pot holing gives me the heebie jeebies, but on the while I would describe myself as claustrophobic.

As I was on the CT bench slowly entering the scanner I did feel a little bit uncomfortable, I was wearing ear muffs as I went in. I was holding onto a buzzer to let the operator know if anything was too much or if the tattoo on my arm started burning.

The scanner made a right racket while I was in there, I asked Mel inside what she thought I should do; obviously the scanner was interfering as she didn't say anything back to me. I felt all alone again and with everything going on I started to have a little cry to myself.

By the time it had completed it cycles of whirring and humming, the bench slid me back out into the open.

In less than an hour I'd have the result of what was going on inside, to say I wasn't ready for the result is an understatement, to say that the changes this little episode of my life was going to have on me was an understatement too.

I was in a position where incarceration for my crimes was a real upcoming prospect, I'd lost people dear to me and was having to deal with the grief of their loss. I was looking at some difficult times ahead for my drink driving.

Now this. Everything was coming undone.

EIGHTY SEVEN

Which brings me to here, where we started, to these four walls.

The doctor has reviewed the CT scan results said that it's unusual to get such a large undiscovered tumour in someone so young; either way, it's too far advanced to even think about operating.

So I'm lying here waiting for the end to come, where you've found me.

I've been released on bail regarding the drink driving, and I suppose there's a part of me waiting for them to return with the results of the DNA search.

Luckily I have my Mel with me, looking after me in the corner, she's just having a read of a book as we speak.

Now there's a couple of further things I need to mention, a brain tumour can have a profound affect on the brain and its thoughts, and what I've said through these pages may not be entirely true.

In fact I've recently undergone a massive psychological trauma, my wife and kids have left me. I lost my job, I was forced to sell my home and live in the squalor of 'bedsit' accommodation.

Sorry, what I mean to say is that I had dabbled in drugs, and, over the years of abuse I had spiralled into an oblivion of paranoia and self disbelief.

No, the truth is that I'm suffering from a mental illness, that didn't manifest itself until my later years, and I haven't taken my medication.

Truth or fabrication? I'm not too sure I can tell you myself, its all become a bit of a haze even for me.

The people you've heard about may never have existed and the things I have done may have just been one of my frequent nightmares, I'm not sure.

One thing is for sure though, and that's that this tumour, eating away at what is left of my brain may be the only real part of all the things I've said, at least it explains all the headaches.

I'll leave it up to you to decide with regards to the truth, being the last person to know what I have or haven't done.

I'm starting to feel a little tired, I think I'm just going to close my eyes for a while...

23419280R00153

Printed in Poland
by Amazon Fulfillment
Poland Sp. z o.o., Wrocław